Country Dying

Also by Robert C. S. Downs

PEOPLES

GOING GENTLY

Country Dying

A Novel by

Robert C. S. Downs

The Bobbs-Merrill Company, Inc.
Indianapolis/New York

Library of Congress Cataloging in Publication Data
Downs, Robert C S
    Country dying.
    I. Title.
PZ4.D7534Co [PS3554.095]   813'.5'4   75-31686
ISBN 0-672-52193-8

For my mother and father

One

The Town

The plan of the town of Oldenfield was very simple. It was as if back in the 1760s some giant ax had torn out a large X in the northern New Hampshire woods. In the middle was the two-story clapboard building that housed both the post office and the postmaster, Moose Krause. Across the street was the town hall, a high straight-back structure that had once looked as beautiful as a church. But it was now an obsolete building, one that was fast decaying. On top of it was a bell tower that had not for many years contained a bell, and what was left of its paint hung from its sides in tightly curled layers. In places its warped gray siding twisted out from its nails as though frozen in some futile escape attempt. The upper left side of the X was the street that led to the Baptist church, the lower side to Millie Barnhope's general store and Simmer's barn, where they kept the fire truck. Little graveled roads sprouted from this main one, forming a small network in among the birch, spruce and pine trees that grew everywhere about the countryside. On the outskirts of town were clearings where houses had once been, most now marked only by a random concrete slab jutting up where a wall had stood. There was a feeling that the town had over many years shrunk in on itself.

All along the two main streets of Oldenfield stood

great houses that had once been beautiful. Some of them were still in good repair, but for the most part it was clear that they had become too much for their owners to maintain. On each house over the front door was the date it had been built: 1776, 1790, 1802, 1812, and so on. But even those that had not been kept up held a certain gracious authority, like grand old ladies who have outlived their incomes. The other houses ranged from one-level ranch homes to outright hovels, most of which were tucked out of sight among the trees. Some of the more pitiful houses leaned precariously to one side, and on the outsides of those still occupied, there were makeshift supports everywhere. The houses looked, in fact, as if they would at any moment separate from their chimneys and go straight to the ground.

And then there were the shacks on the mountain just north of town. Only one road went up the mountain, but even a careful observer could not see the shacks because of the number of cords of firewood that surrounded them. Of the three men who lived on the mountain, two were hermits; and one, Bony James, was a near-hermit who came down to Oldenfield only to tend the cemetery and dig the graves. All three farmed a little produce from the rocky hardpan, but during the endless gray days of late winter and early spring their diet consisted mainly of bread and the better grades of canned dogfood. There were a few trees—skinny, thinned-out pines—on the very top of the mountain, and in them and the way they stood was the history of all the weather that had ever crossed the mountain. Like a line of withered, beaten soldiers bent against some invisible enemy, they leaned in unison away from the wind that never stopped, that seemed in fact never to slow up at all.

The other main street in Oldenfield was really a loop road that connected at both ends with Route 10, a state road in such poor condition that March that in places it was almost impassable. The frost heaves had broken down into jagged ulcers in the pavement, and there was great fear in the town that a thaw and then a hard freeze would cut them off completely from Newfield and the other nearby towns. There was also a fear that the state was going to make an assessment on the town in order to repair the road, and wherever groups of townspeople gathered there was endless speculation on what the cost would be. In the beginning there was much resistance to the idea of an assessment, but as the road deteriorated through January and February the people began to know that there was no real alternative to whatever the state wanted to do. What helped them arrive at that decision was the simple fact that the state had neither answered nor acknowledged any of the requests for spring maintenance. Still, every Monday the proper forms went out from the town clerk.

Culver

Culver Thomas was the only one of six young men from Oldenfield to return from World War II, and he had come back on crutches, a hobbling wreck of a man. In front of town hall on a fiercely hot July 4, 1945, he had been elected town clerk by voice vote. The job paid $1,800 a year, and with his disability pay the town had secured his future. During the next four years he had six operations on his right leg to piece together the ligaments and tendons shattered by nineteen pieces of shrapnel.

Culver's activities the first few years after he came back from the war were a permanent part of town legend. Still on his crutches he had married, as town talk went, "one of them USO things," and she had come to Oldenfield from just outside Birmingham, Alabama. She arrived in the town standing among three large steamer trunks in the back of Culver's '47 pickup. Five months later she left the same way, her head held high, her brown hair streaming in the wind behind her. Culver, at the wheel, looking like a crazed man, made the five-mile trip to the depot in Newfield in less than five minutes.

In those days Culver drank bourbon in a way that had the townspeople agreeing that their clerk was on his way to an early grave. It was not uncommon in the town to be awakened well past midnight by Culver trying to get to his house and, along the way, recounting a dandy war story to any tree that barred his path. But the event that seriously threatened his next election happened the year after he had rid himself of his first wife. He made Volunteer Day, a weekend fair and the most important town event of the year, a disaster for all. Swinging one crutch while balancing on the other, he had cleaned off the two cakes tables and was heading for the relish displays when Ned Hoffer, the first and only policeman in town, kicked his crutches out from under him.

That year Culver was reelected by a margin of three votes, 112–109, and it was then that he began to change. It was as though his youth had simply run out of him. He stopped drinking and did his leg exercises faithfully, and for the first time in his life he realized he was lonely. It was then that he got his first dog, and from then on he did not really measure his life in years but in the dogs he owned. On days when he could go without his crutches for several hours, he worked in the largest but worst-kept garden in town or, in the cold months, did small carpentry tasks in the L that connected the house with the barn. As his leg got better he began to hunt with his dog: first rabbits in the pastures behind the house, then crows, and finally deer on the mountain.

Year by year his election margin increased, and the year he married Ellen Niles from Newfield he got all the town votes except the twelve Democrats'.

The following spring he went to work for Ellen's father, building houses in Newfield. When Mr. Niles died two years later Culver took over the business, and the money he got from it he put into buying the land between Oldenfield and the mountain. He assembled the tract the way some people work on giant puzzles, and when he was finished he owned almost eight hundred acres.

He was by then well on his way to becoming wealthy, and there was talk of his running for the state legislature, when his son and only child was crushed to death by a bulldozer. Culver was thirty-nine when it happened, and Ellen thirty-five. It was an event that made Culver almost instantly old. But somehow through the years he began to get over it; somehow he found a way to accommodate it; and by the time he was fifty-two his belly was puffed out over his belt, his hair was nearly all gone, and his cheeks and jaw were in permanent sag. His eyes, though, still held a kind of unexplained joy, as though his army days were still alive, and his mouth curled at the right corner in a way that suggested he alone possessed some fine secret.

But Ellen Thomas never really recovered from her son's death, and through the years she came to put most of her energy and all of her affection into the Baptist church. Where previously she and Culver had attended perhaps once a month, they now went regularly, and within a year after her son's death Ellen was the Reverend Mr. Barker's right arm. She also became the soloist of the five-man choir on Sundays, and daily she moved about the house singing and humming her hymns.

In the late afternoons Culver listened to Ellen rehearse, looking at her and recalling what parts of her had been visible in his son's face. Then before dinner Culver would sit in his chair by the window and look out at the town going down under the twilight. There was a brief, special time in the early evening when Culver could see the town settle into a kind of blue anesthesia, and from his window he could look into the distance and watch the final daylight as it played for a few minutes in the mists that rose from the dump just west of town. Then the little village would begin to define itself against the night, and Culver could almost hear the forty or so kitchen lights smacking to life. Then the chimney fires, at first white broom handles against the blue-black sky, soon snapped out their sparks and turned to true smoke.

The March morning when Culver got the certified letter from the state broke clear and bright. The night had been hollow and quietly still, but when the sun was finally up, it was not long before the huge icicles on the houses were dripping in their own special rhythms. As he walked to the post office, Culver saw where the snow cover was beginning to sag in the pastures behind the houses, and little circles of brown grass were already spreading at the bases of the taller trees.

Moose Krause was waiting for him, the letter in his hand. "State's finally taken some notice," Moose said from in back of the little window. He pushed the yellow receipt at Culver, who signed it and slid it back. "With them chuckholes as bad as that, it's a man's own hell just getting to Newfield and back," Moose went on. Culver turned the letter in his hand and began to open it. "Barnhope boy drove his snow machine smack into Prior Lake last night. Busted up an ankle, Millie said. Machine's a goner."

Culver lifted his eyes slowly from the letter and let them stay for a moment on Moose's face. "There ought to be a season on snow machines," Culver said. "Just about as long as there is on deer." He folded the letter and put it into his jacket pocket.

"They going to fix up them chuckholes?" Moose asked. He nodded at Culver's middle.

"They don't say anything about it," Culver answered.

He turned and walked to the large bulletin board,

which was covered with announcements and notices of all varieties. He stood in front of it for several minutes as his eyes moved over the fliers on barn sales, church suppers in Newfield and towns farther away, and the seemingly endless auctions. Then his eyes fell on the paper he had put up four weeks before which announced the day of town meeting. Under "Agenda, Business from the Floor," he carefully wrote in capitals: "ITEM 1: MR. FRANKLIN SORENSON, ASSISTANT TO THE DIRECTOR OF HIGHWAY DEVELOPMENT."

As soon as he was out the door, Moose came out from the back to read what he had written. To everyone who came for mail that morning he proudly announced that the state was readying to fix the chuckholes. By noon his story was that the trucks were probably already on their way.

The letter inside Culver's jacket felt like a heavy stone. There was something indescribably gray about it, something untouchable in the wording. In its formal language it requested Culver, as town clerk, to reserve time at the town meeting so that, as the letter said, "there may ensue reasonable discussion of the future of highway development in the Granite State."

Outside, the day that had seemed full of promise, that had broken with a clear eastern light, was already fading into the grays of a New England morning in early spring. Looking up toward the mountain as he walked, Culver saw it slip almost imperceptibly into one of its many different moods. The early morning mists that rose up from the valley had already burned off, and for a moment it seemed that the mountain would resist the low dumb clouds just off to the east. But then, quickly, the mountain was gone.

Millie

Not only was Millie Barnhope large enough to look like a bully, but frequently she acted like one. She was, as she put it herself, "sole owner, sole clerk, sole goddamn everything" of the Oldenfield general store. The sign above the small flat building said TOWN STORE, and painted in right after it in her own hand was & NURSERY. Millie ran the store with a power and energy that seemed to bubble up from some well deep inside her. Her day began at seven in the morning, and often she was busy past nine o'clock at night. But she showed fatigue only after the last customer had left, when she was able to retreat to the three rooms in the back of the store. Each night she would take a six-pack from the cooler, tuck it into the crook of her arm like a precious football, and go either to the comfort and warmth of the Franklin stove in the back or to the nine-by-nine greenhouse she had built just off the kitchen. In either case, within an hour she would be asleep by the stove, her feet straight out before her, pointing at the dying reds in the fire.

Millie had been in Oldenfield only eight years, and it was remarkable that the store had survived at all. It was as if she had simply willed it to live, and things for her and her fourteen-year-old son had been desperate during the first year. For eighteen years before coming to Oldenfield she and her husband had run a similar but much larger store in Connecticut. Millie attributed his death to the fact that, as she put it, "the withered old bastard just couldn't take it anymore." She had tried to run the store by herself, but quickly it had proved much too large for her, and she had sold out and come north to Oldenfield looking for a smaller, more compact business.

At the end of the first year she counted twelve regular

8

customers and perhaps another five or six who bought only beer and cigarettes. She had three thousand dollars left, and as winter settled in that year there was no clear prospect of making the store a success. If asked that first December how many friends she had made, she would quite properly have responded, "One—Moose Krause." And it was he who told her the reason the store had not yet succeeded. "Oldenfield ain't Connecticut," Moose had said with a kind of satisfied arrogance. "Not by a long shot."

"I'm a good storekeeper," Millie told him. "And a damned honest person."

"The problem's time," Moose went on.

"I've been here one whole year," she said with bewilderment.

"Which in this town is maybe twenty minutes."

But she had survived the winter, if only just barely, and in the spring the townspeople had begun to come to the store. As if each had given her a test, they came one by one, first to buy an item or two, then a few days' supplies. Just after Easter, Carl Simmer, the only selectman in Oldenfield, phoned in an order for a week's groceries, and from then on Millie's survival was assured. But it was a full three years before anyone ever called her anything but Mrs. Barnhope.

All the time that Culver was in the post office that morning, Millie sat in her jeep opening the handful of monthly bills. She kept up a constant stream of private abuse for each of the bills, carrying in her mind their totals and putting them against her current monthly tally. When she finally put them down on the seat next to her and looked up, she saw Culver heading off toward his house. As she watched him walk into the distance, she thought there seemed something sad and heavy about him, and she glanced from him back to the post office, as if she might find the answer there. Just as she was about to start the jeep, Moose Krause came out the front door of the building. She rolled down the window as he came toward her. "Now don't you go telling anybody I told you this," he said, "but them chuckholes is getting fixed."

"Says who?"

"Culver got the letter from the highway people," Moose said. "I saw it myself."

"One more quick freeze on that road," Millie said, "and they'll have to close it off. Then where'll we all be?"

"I'm telling you," Moose went on.

Millie thought for a moment and then gave a soft little grunt, as though she had finally accepted the fact. "Maybe if they get that road going, my sign'll bring in the transients," she said. "You know that sign cost me thirty-five dollars?"

Moose moved his hand along the side of the door, and with his thumbnail he chipped away some ice. "Things're thin," he finally said.

Millie picked up the pile of bills and held them out to him. "Not in seven years have I been in the red," she said, partly to Moose, partly to the bills. "Not until this month." She held the bills for a moment and then began to shake them with a great anger. "Now Millie Barnhope has creditors crawling up both arms."

"They fix up them chuckholes, things'll be all right," Moose told her. He patted the door as if to comfort it.

"There was a hundred fifty people here ten years ago," Millie said suddenly. "A hundred fifty. I could live off that." She looked away through the windshield, and for just an instant her eyes became frantic and distant. "And now what the hell have we got?"

"Eighty-seven," Moose said.

"Eighty-six if old man Keller finally croaked off last night," she said without looking at him. They both gave pathetic little laughs, and then Millie looked at Moose

and said, "I got to go see my boy." As she started to back
out of the post office Moose called to her, "You got any
import beer in?"

"Cases of it," she yelled as she drove off.

Moose

The arrangement Moose Krause had with the postal
service was ideal. He owned the building and leased
space to the government. In the agreement he had nego-
tiated, the government would pay all the utilities for the
first floor. The heat was certainly no problem; Moose
simply turned it up at night, and it kept the upper floor
of the building very comfortable. The electrical wiring
had taken only a small degree of rerouting, and for years
Moose had lived free off the government. His salary was
a good one, and he had saved nearly nineteen thousand
dollars in the thirty years he had been postmaster. But
in no way did that money compensate for the losses he
had suffered. At fifty-five it was as though some spiritual
shotgun had blown away most of his soul. He was a
haggard, restless man who thrived on rumor and town
dirt, a man who was a conspicuous failure to everyone
but himself. He had been especially so to his wife, a
woman who had endured him for thirty-one years and,
so rumor had it, was about to go and live with her sister
in Vermont when she dropped dead in the A&P in Newfield. Somehow, though, Moose never suspected that he
was anything but the most important person in town; a
sayer of wise things; an authority on weather and hunting; a clever, crafty person.

Moose had not lost his teeth gracefully. As they fell out
over a period of seven years, his face collapsed inward
under his nose like the lower portion of a building being
sucked in. His eyes bulged more and more, showing far
more white than blue, and his cheeks thinned out

steadily until they suddenly one day collapsed along his jawbones. His whole face looked, in fact, the reverse of that of the giant Canadian moose that hung on the post office wall between the brownish photographs of the President and the Postmaster General. The trophy was Moose's prize possession, the spoils of a hunting trip almost twenty-five years earlier and the source of his permanent nickname. But, like almost everything else in and around the post office, it was in what seemed the last stages of its existence.

Moose had two children, neither of whom he had seen for over ten years, or since just after his wife died; but that did not stop him from inventing stories of their great success which he passed on to all. Although he knew nothing about them or even their whereabouts, to the people in Oldenfield they were both married; one lived in Massachusetts, the other in Maine; his son was a pharmacist, his daughter a schoolteacher. In response to whether he was a grandfather, Moose would always reply, "Now we're a-hoping, we are."

His children had nothing to do with him for a very simple reason: when they were little he had beaten them mercilessly for the slightest infraction of the household laws he had set up. They were awful beatings that kept the children out of school for several days. When he beat them he screamed and howled abuses at them, as if he were trying to drive some demon out of himself.

When the children finally left Oldenfield after high school, Moose tried one night to beat his wife. With a hunting knife she put a wound in his left arm that took forty stitches to close. From then on, when Moose would begin one of his rages, his wife would tell him that if he ever so much as put a finger to her she'd cut him into pieces so small that he wouldn't even make good sparrow feed.

After she died, and after the children were gone for good, Moose seemed somehow to mellow into real middle age, acting in a way that suggested the demons inside him had dissolved, had simply melted away and gone.

"I was heading down behind Simmer's Garage," Jerky Barnhope said to his mother, "and I was cutting it real good. Had her open about fifty, fifty-five. Route Ten was clear, clear both ways—I could see that."

"You're a punk," Millie said to him. Her eyes ran over the thick cast that went all the way to his knee. "You know what that machine cost?" Jerky fixed his gaze about the middle of her neck, and his whole face suddenly became vacant. There were several stitches in a random pattern on his face where the ice on the lake had splintered and cut him up in quick little flashes. "I didn't even have it paid for," she told him.

"It was one of them chuckholes," Jerky said. "I swear it was. It must have been a new one; it had to be. Going across the road it jammed the steering, threw the track all to hell. It ain't but twenty yards from Simmer's to the lake. I mean, what the hell could I do?"

"See if you can get your pants on over that," she said to the cast. "I got to get back to the store."

Jerky turned slightly on the edge of the bed and looked at the chair near the door where his clothes lay in a neat little pile. He looked at the olive-drab army fatigues with a mixture of security and terrible hate. There were small dark bloodstains on the jacket and pants from where the ice had cut him, and the brim of the fatigue hat was bent back like a child's baseball cap. The thigh pockets of the trousers bulged with all he cared about in the world: a knife, six cartridges for his 30.06 rifle, his deck of cards for solitaire, some souvenir paper money from Vietnam, and the yellow tobacco pouch that held his marijuana.

As he struggled into his trousers, he felt for each of the items and was relieved to find that no one had taken anything.

Millie watched him wiggle about on the edge of the bed as he slowly dressed himself, and then suddenly in a vicious burst of anger she said, "When in hell are you going to do something with yourself?"

"When the time comes," he said.

"Home eighteen months and you ain't done a damned thing."

"There isn't anything to do," he said. He picked up his left boot and began to lace it.

Millie picked up the right one and held it close to her with both hands as though it were some strange delicate vase. "You could do something at the store," she said. "Something in the greenhouse."

"Screw the store," Jerky said. "Did anyone pull my machine out?"

"Simmer said it was totaled," Millie told him. "He said he'd give me twenty-five bucks on it."

"Screw Simmer," Jerky said. He eased himself away from the bed and balanced himself on his left foot. He leaned over and took the crutches from the chair and slipped them under his arms. Then he moved quickly and easily out the door and on down the hall.

Jerky

Nearly twenty-three when he came back to Oldenfield from Vietnam, Jerky Barnhope had no particular sense of values or, for that matter, reality. As the plane lifted off the runway, Jerky had promised himself two things: that he would be as kind to people as he possibly could, and that he would stay high for as much of the rest of his life as he could.

The first promise broke down shortly after he got home. The second, even after a year and a half, was still very much intact. The first promise was broken because, for most of the people in Oldenfield, coming back from

Vietnam was more of a test than going. People in the town waited for him to be like the young people they watched on television, and Jerky did not disappoint them.

Still, there were those who tried to help him. Culver Thomas offered to get him a job building houses in Newfield; Moose Krause said he needed an assistant in the post office; and The Reverend Mr. Barker offered him the job of part-time sexton. Jerky got high.

In her own blunt motherly way Millie was very proud of Jerky, and she was also very relieved that he had survived combat without wounds. But even her patience had run short after he had been back six months and had done absolutely nothing except lie in his bed in his fatigues, drive his snow machine, and walk around the store glassy-eyed. All her attempts to talk to him were met with a vacant, empty stare, as if his mind when called upon to think of the war would shrink into itself like some scared flower. When after a time this had happened repeatedly, Millie resigned herself to the fact that he had become worthless. She decided that he had had too much experience for a boy his age. One night she even asked him about the women he had met in Vietnam, and he answered, "Slants, nothing but yellow little slants. Just as soon kill them as look at them."

Then, as though she had been warming up to it, Millie said, "What's that smell coming out of your room all the time?"

"Grass."

"Do you know what would happen if Ned Hoffer knew you had that crap?"

"Sure," Jerky said. "He'd come busting in here and try to take it. Then he'd arrest me, or try to."

"He could close up the store."

"He tries to take my stuff and I'll kill him," Jerky said.

Looking at him, Millie realized with great horror that Jerky not only would do it, but that he could. From then on she did not ask him questions about Vietnam or the war. She kept him at a spiritual arm's length, half-terrified of what he might someday do, half-proud in her own way that he actually knew how to kill.

But for Jerky, most of his activities, his language, his public attitudes were part of a mask. He saw himself as an increasingly delicate web inside an ever hardening shell. At night he often would get up and go to the bathroom and stand for a very long time looking into the mirror. In eighteen months he had neither cut his hair nor shaved. His hair was curling down past his shoulders in chunky waves; he was very proud of its length. But his beard had been a dismal failure. His sideburns seemed to have run out of growing strength, stopping more or less of their own accord halfway down his cheek. His moustache, which he had hoped would be a Fu Manchu, was so thinned out that it looked pasted on. A few soft brown curls hung limply from his chin. He would run his hand over his face and smile at the seemingly random growth of hair. Then he would go back to his room, carefully pack and roll a joint, and smoke it in a hard and furious way. After a few minutes he would turn and look out the window of his room onto the small pond and narrow stream that ran just past the back of the store. When he had just returned from the war, the landscape behind the house was to him an awesome network of the unknown. Disconnected and floating from the marijuana, Jerky would sit on the bed cross-legged and stare into the blackness, sometimes quite beautifully lighted by the moon, and see guerrillas so magnificently camouflaged that to shoot them was to shoot the foliage itself. Sometimes, especially in the beginning, he would replay the fire-fights he had been in, the murders and killings he had seen and done. He saw children as delicate as drawings from fairy tales blow themselves up, and others, their faces contorted and insanely vicious, kill with a professionalism so perfect that Jerky knew it had been taught to them before they could walk. And on many nights the omnipotent tanks came out of the tall pine forest not more than fifty yards from his window, blowing the gentle oxen out of their swamps just for the pleasure of watching the great passive animals explode.

But that was in the beginning when after several joints Jerky could not even tell where he was. Now, a year and a half later, when he looked out on the pond and little stream, there was no battlefield; he saw only a profound harmony and peace in the nighttime landscape. He wished sometimes during those nights that his mother would come into his room so that he could tell her how much he loved her, how he loved all that he saw, how in the hard daylight love soured into a pity for all humanity. He wished desperately to tell someone the true dimension of his love, to be able to articulate the blue flowing emotions that swept through him. Often after a long time of looking out toward the woods he would utter aloud, "I have this love."

The Newfield hospital was not more than a stone's throw from Route 10, and Millie braked cautiously as she turned the jeep onto the road. Before shifting she looked at the surface of the road just in front of her, and then her eyes moved slowly, picking their way, for several hundred feet. "Worse and worse every day," she said as she jogged the jeep around the chuckholes. To Jerky the chuckholes looked like craters that had been made by toy bombs. Millie turned half toward her son and said, "Moose Krause said the state's coming to fix up this mess of a road."

"It's all right the way it is," Jerky answered.

"You're going to pay for the snowmobile," Millie said through her teeth.

"I know I am," he answered.

"You're not going to put yourself to work now, are you?"

"I'm going to stick up Simmer's Garage," Jerky said.

When Millie pulled the jeep into the dirt area in front of her store, Carl Simmer was waiting in his truck. Millie was out of the jeep before Jerky, and Simmer came around the end of his truck with his hand already held out. "I've brought along the twenty-five dollars," he said to Millie.

Jerky came around the side of the truck on his crutches and said, "Go suck on an exhaust pipe."

"It's up to you," Simmer told him. He rubbed the money around in his hand.

"What's it going to cost to fix my machine?" Jerky asked.

"I can't rightly say," Simmer told him, "but I ain't got the time and I ain't got the parts."

"You fix up my machine."

"You take the twenty-five and count yourself lucky."

Jerky started to lean toward Simmer, and Millie saw his anger bulging his neck veins. "You're a cheap son of a bitch," Jerky said. Simmer smiled at him with great disdain and then handed the money to Millie, who took it and put it in the pocket of her ski parka. "I'll kill you, you son of a bitch," Jerky said, but Simmer had already turned and was getting back into his truck. "Do you hear me, you bastard?" Jerky yelled as the motor banged alive. He hobbled toward the door of the truck. "Do you hear me?" he screamed.

Simmer backed the truck up a few feet and then stopped short. With his elbow out the window he said, somewhat as if he were starting up a whole new conversation, "I always been meaning to ask you. You ever kill anybody when you was over there?"

Jerky's face went instantly flat and white; his whole body stiffened with the question. He looked past Simmer and off somewhere beyond the truck and the store.

"I didn't think so," Simmer said, and he eased the truck into gear and was gone.

Simmer

Carl Simmer was the most popular and the most powerful person in Oldenfield. In the 1940s during the heavy gas rationing he had obligated many people to him. In some strange and mysterious way he always had a plentiful supply of gas, and he told all the people in Oldenfield that the government really had plenty of gas: the rationing of it was to save the rubber on their tires. But if you were from Newfield and you came to Simmer's Garage looking for gas, you never even got him to come out of the building to ask you what you wanted.

Shortly after V-J Day, Simmer was elected unopposed to the Board of Selectmen. In 1955 one of the other two members of the board died, and four years later the other one retired and went to live with his children in Newfield. No one in the town ever suggested that they be replaced, and for the last thirteen years Carl Simmer had run the town by himself.

He was a handsome, rugged-looking man with a great blanket of white hair pulled straight back from his forehead. His face was always red, as though he had just finished exerting himself, and although his work was exclusively in and around the gas station, he was extraordinarily clean. When he would take money for gas, his hands looked as immaculate as a priest's. His clothes were always carefully laundered, and never had he been seen either in town or in his garage without a necktie, which was always ballooned out just a trifle over the top of his overalls.

There were two other things about him that seemed somehow to set him off from the ordinary: his smile and his voice. His smile was a kind of town event, his broad square face suddenly opening into a warmth that made all present feel as though they were on the verge of making a lifelong friend. His voice had the same quality to it, and anyone to whom he spoke had the instant feeling that Simmer was concerned exclusively with that person's total well-being.

But perhaps more than the people in the town, Simmer loved the idea of Oldenfield. That was true because he had never in his life known anything else. Born there in the early 1900s, Simmer had never been out of the state of New Hampshire, and in his way he was fiercely proud of the fact. His life had been almost completely the town and his garage, and the only things he knew better than the people of Oldenfield were their cars.

He could have been a wealthy man; certainly enough money had gone through his hands, but he had spent almost all of it on the town itself. He had put a wing on The Reverend Mr. Barker's church for Sunday school classes; he had bought outright from the state the land and the school building where most of Oldenfield had gone to school, but which now stood empty and useless; and he had built two war memorials for those from the town who had died in both world wars. And each year he made large contributions to maintain all that he had sponsored. In addition, he maintained the fire truck, paid for the printing of the town report, and during the last five years had quietly assumed the maintenance of the town hall. He had no family.

When Simmer got back from Millie's store, Culver was sitting in his pickup beside the gas pump. Simmer pulled alongside and leaned over to roll down the window. "You want gas?" he called.

"You got any?"

"Some."

Culver smiled a little and said, "How's five gallons?"

"Can do," Simmer said as he got out of his truck. "But not from the pumps. It's inside."

Without speaking, the two men walked into the large wooden building and entered the office on the left side. The right side of the building was a huge two-story structure that only four months before had berthed four cars at a time. Now it stood empty except for Jerky Barnhope's snow machine, which sat all bent and twisted in the path of the huge blower that hummed its heat over the whole place. Jerky's face mask hung from the right handlebar and swayed slowly in the dry, bilious heat. Simmer and Culver went into the garage area and walked slowly to the hundred-gallon kerosene tank in the back. Culver watched as Simmer began to pump gasoline into a five-gallon Shell can, and after a moment he said, "Where'd you get all the gas?"

"One of the drivers, the old one, he ain't afraid of that goddamn road," Simmer said, without looking up. He eased the can off the little spigot and set it down at Culver's feet. Then he looked up and said, "Moose Krause said you got notice on the road this morning."

"He would," Culver replied, shaking his head. "When they were handing out brains . . . ," he started to say, and then he stopped and looked at Simmer. "There was a letter saying a Mr. Sorenson was coming to town meeting. It says he's from the highway people."

"Think he'll do the assessing?"

"Or tell us it's got to be done," Culver answered.

There was a short silence between them, and then Simmer finally asked, "What do you figure on?"

"A hundred, a hundred and a half a head."

"People are talking maybe twenty-five dollars," Simmer said.

"Keeping that road open is going to cost ten, maybe twelve thousand."

"There's some'll have a time of it at a hundred dollars," Simmer told him.

Culver looked away and his eyes landed on Jerky's snow machine. "What are you going to do with that?" he asked.

"Want to buy it?"

"Be serious."

"Junk it for the parts."

"To look at it, it's a wonder the boy didn't kill himself," Culver said.

"Wouldn't have been no great loss if he had," Simmer said.

"Any word on Keller?"

"Not this morning," Simmer answered, a sudden veil over his face. "Can't be long now, though," he went on. "Never is when Barker starts visiting a sick house twice a day."

"Not a funeral all winter."

"Can't be long."

Culver pulled his hat down and picked up the Shell can from the floor. "They want us to go higher than a hundred," he said, "and they'll have a pack of trouble."

Two

In earlier years the town meeting had been a jubilant affair that lasted from noon to midnight. It had been the event of the year: a time for the town to shake itself up, to hang out all its dirty laundry; a time for true orators, a place for the real town wits to battle.

No longer was it any of these. The town meeting was now only a skeleton of the great body of tradition and meaning it had once been. The great debates were gone for good, the spitfire exchanges now only dim echoes from people grown dim and shadowy themselves. Instead of the crushing one-liners that brought the house down, there was now sarcasm; instead of the shouts that would turn a speaker purple, there were now only private grumbles. But the form of the meeting was still exactly the same: Simmer moderated, and Culver was in charge of the town report and the elections, which in past years had been the highlight of the day. But now even these had lost their excitement, even their dignity, and instead of real and fervent contests, the elections had become habit and routine. The problem, really, was that at town meeting there was no longer any fun. But the people of Oldenfield still prepared for it as if they were going away for a long weekend.

At ten minutes before noon, almost as if the long-vanished bell on top of the town hall were ringing, the people began to come out of their houses and funnel toward the center of town. With as much ceremony as possible, Simmer and Culver stood on the steps of the building and greeted all as they came. Everyone in the town was there except the Kellers and Ned Hoffer, and when the front section of the hall was filled, Simmer and Culver took their places at a long table on the small wooden stage. To the left side of the stage an old American flag hung in the shadows, and to the right the state flag of New Hampshire drooped in a tattered mirror image.

When Simmer rose, there was immediate silence. "I declare the two hundred and twelfth meeting of the town of Oldenfield, county of Mellingford, state of New Hampshire, to be in session. The Reverend Mr. Barker will lead us in prayer. No smoking."

Mr. Barker rose slowly from the front row and half-turned toward the people. "We implore God's guidance and direction in the business before us this day. Amen."

"Thank you, Mr. Barker," Simmer said directly on the heels of the "Amen." "The first business of the day will be the reading of the town report by Mr. Culver Thomas."

Although Culver had the right to read the report, he had never done so. He always limited himself to the town census for the year, and then he called on each of the individuals who had prepared a specific section of the report. He rose slowly, the report open like a slim hymn-book in his hands, and read, "Births last year: none. Deaths: seven. Population for the town of Oldenfield, New Hampshire, as of this date: eighty-seven."

He closed the little pamphlet and looked out over the people. What he saw in that moment was a hall only a third full, the people seemingly huddled near the front as though seeking some kind of shelter, and he remembered for an instant when the whole place had been filled to its walls with all the people he had ever known in Oldenfield, squatting in the front, standing in rows along the sides, sometimes so tightly packed that in places they looked as if they were sitting two to a chair. Then he said, "Mr. Harold Bitterley for the Volunteers."

Bitterley was a thin, withered old man who, although not quite sixty, looked at least ten years older. Years before, he had been one of the town's great orators, and always at town meeting the people had looked forward to his speeches on the current condition of state government. But in the last few years it seemed that an early senility had begun to stuff up his jugulars, and his speeches and attempts to carry on his grand days were now always cut short.

He rose from his seat on the side and turned to face the small crowd. For a moment his body puffed up, and in the way he held himself it seemed that he would launch forth once again into a moving and hilarious speech. When he began, though, it was immediately clear that his voice was suddenly much older than his body, and it carried with it only an invitation to ridicule.

" 'Tis for me a great and significant pleasure . . . ," he began, then stopped and fumbled with the report. It was as though someone had let the air out of his body. He opened the booklet and began to read what he had written down. "The place of the volunteer fire department within the community of Oldenfield is crucial," he said. For an instant he seemed confused. From the middle of the crowd came, "Just the figures, Hal, just the figures. Ain't nobody got all day."

In a low, defeated voice he read, " 'Brush fires: seven; chimney fires: two; burned-outs: one, Mrs. Canning. Three hundred seventy miles on the pumper.' "

"Request for increase in mileage rate?" Simmer asked.

"No request," Bitterley answered. He sat down in the wooden chair, put his elbows across his knees, and stared at the dirty floor.

"Calvin Runners," Culver called.

Runners was so fat that he seemed to be bubbling up and out of his clothes. He got to his feet slowly, the town report sandwiched between his fat pink hands. He opened it and read: " 'Three requests for easements last year,' " then went on to say what the first two were and why they had been denied. Then he said, "Millie Barnhope's petition for an easement to raise a sign for her place of business on town land adjacent to Route Ten was approved." He sat heavily in his chair, relieved.

Culver got up and said that because of Ned Hoffer's being in the hospital in Newfield he'd read the constable's report. " 'House calls: two; road calls: two. No crimes, no arrests. Seven hundred twelve miles on the vehicle.' "

The meeting went on for a long time; the other areas of the town report were covered methodically. What little calling out there was at the beginning of the meeting soon dropped off, and here and there among the crowd some of the older people napped. At three o'clock Culver, declaring the reading of the town report to be at an end, announced an adjournment by saying, "Town officers to be elected at three-thirty prompt."

Almost immediately the hall emptied. Outside, the people stood in small groups talking town rumor and speculating on the cost of the state assessment for the repair of Route 10. Some drank from thermoses; others took snacks from brown paper bags.

Simmer and Culver came out together and stood near the street on a worn brown patch of ground that would never again support growth of any kind. When they stopped, it was as though they saw the car simultaneously. What repelled them immediately was its standardization: Chevrolet station wagon, white, the state seal like a gaudy heraldic badge on the door. Around it in a neat circle was the green lettering that said, "Department of Highways." At the wheel, looking straight ahead, sat Mr. Franklin Sorenson.

"Looks like the state fellow," Simmer said. As though moved by some giant hand, Culver walked to the car. He had to tap on the window to get Sorenson's attention. "Now you're going to have to wait," Culver said through the glass. "We still got our elections to go yet."

Sorenson looked at his watch and then gazed down the road ahead of him. Culver watched him mouth the words, "Very good," and then he turned and walked back to Simmer.

"What's he like?" Simmer asked quietly.

"Can't tell," Culver answered, as though talking to himself.

"Worst kind."

Sorenson

Franklin Sorenson detested anything that was old. He was the sort of man who would have junked the Liberty Bell because it was cracked. He loved things like steel, chrome and plastic, and had a fierce dislike for anything not man-made. He lived in a squared-off one-bedroom apartment just outside Concord, the state capital. Although the buildings and houses in Concord had a certain charm because of their age, Sorenson had nearly gone crazy living in the ground-floor apartment of the Victorian house he had rented when first coming to Concord twelve years before. He had hated its curves, its long hallways, its total individuality. So he was among the first renters in the modular two-story apartment complex; in fact, he had gotten his money down before ground had been broken. What had sold him was the plan of the complex: everything was marvelously on square, perfectly proportioned; all dimensions within the complex were divisible by a factor of four. He felt an immeasurable comfort when he looked at the plans; the solid squares and rectangles of the drawings were to him the very essence of beauty. He seemed to find in the tight geometry of the building something he had been looking for all his life.

And Sorenson took meticulous care of his apartment. He was concerned with cleanliness to a degree far beyond what might make for humor. With utter ruthlessness he worked nightly on a certain set task in a way that hinted he was trying to clean something he could not get his hands on. Inside the front door precisely at eye level was a list of daily chores which had for its title, "YOUR RESPONSIBILITIES." It read:

Monday: Wash/wax all uncarpeted square footage
Tuesday: Criss-cross vacuuming
Wednesday: Appliances, major/minor
Thursday: Criss-cross vacuuming
Friday: Bathroom
Sat/Sun: Disinfection/pest control

If Sorenson's private life was absurdly compulsive, his professional life was a masterpiece of control and efficiency. While he was an expert in highway cost maintenance and right-of-way acquisitions, his knowledge was not confined to abstractions. He knew how to operate every piece of heavy machinery he had ever seen, and when he was in the field it was common for him to literally toss an operator from the seat of his cab and take over. He was a doer, a man who thrived on seeing daily progress in whatever he supervised, and although he was not an unreasonable man to work for, nobody stood around and shot the breeze when Sorenson was there.

But Sorenson had one problem, and he knew that it was fast becoming a major one in his life. He had a temper that was like a blowtorch—one minute it was just gas, the next a deadly and destructive thing. He knew that in the last three years, or since shortly after he had turned forty, it was less and less under control. There seemed to be in him a little volcano that over the years had begun to boil and moan ever more insistently. Where certain remarks people made had in the past dropped from his skin as if it were armor, they now slipped inside and stung his soft and rubbery soul. He reacted now where several years ago he had not. At first he had lashed out with words, torrents of them streaming from his mouth, but in the last two years there had been two instances when he had actually struck a subordinate. He had not just landed one punch; he had tried to kill the other man. Some said that if he had not been so out of control he probably would have. Because of these two episodes, Sorenson had been passed over for promotion.

In his living room was a huge map of the state of New Hampshire, with miniature flags jutting from the towns where Sorenson had worked for the Highway Department. There were two and three flags around some of the larger towns, and before he left his apartment on the morning of the town meeting in Oldenfield, he had put a new flag into the map.

Because the number of seconding speeches was unlimited, the town elections took a long time. Often, the meeting was the only opportunity for people in the town to get things off their chests. They were far more interested in the seconding speeches than in the elections.

When the adjournment ended, Culver rose from his seat and said, "The election of the Keeper shall be first. Who now supports Mrs. Arnold Keller in her effort?" Several people routinely seconded her nomination. "Who in addition seeks this post?" When there was no answer Culver said, "Seconding testimonies for Mrs. Keller."

There were four seconding speeches, none of which

had anything to do with supporting Mrs. Keller. Two concerned opposite views of the tax rate, one complained about the slowness of snow removal during one of the storms in January, and the last had as its main point the pollution of Potter Stream, one of Prior Lake's main tributaries, by the sewer system in Newfield. This last speech was given by Hal Bitterley, and when he called the condition a "defecation on the area," Simmer banged his gavel and said, "That'll do for now." Directly after, Mrs. Keller was elected Keeper of the Town History for the thirty-third time.

The procedure was repeated over and over until all the town officers had been reelected. Then Culver rose to say that the main business of the meeting was concluded, and that now the town would be pleased to receive Mr. Franklin Sorenson, Assistant to the Director of Highways.

As if on cue, Sorenson entered from the back of the hall and came down the center aisle. In his left hand he carried a large map case that nearly dragged along the floor. In his right hand, swaying back and forth as he walked, was an apparatus that looked like a portable movie screen. He went up the four little steps to the right of the stage and came quickly across to the small table where Simmer and Culver sat. With his back to the audience, he set the case down next to the table and leaned the awkward tripod against it. He looked at Culver and then to the tripod and said, "Erect the stand, please."

Like an obedient schoolboy Culver moved to do so, and when he had it in place he stood beside it as though awaiting further instructions. It was only then that Sorenson took off his hat and overcoat and turned to face the people. He looked at once awesome and silly. His dark blue three-piece suit made him look like a banker who had suddenly been dropped into a poolroom. The suit was perfectly cut, and his necktie was so perfectly aligned that it looked starched. Across his middle was a gold watch chain that made a long thin moustache as it curved up between the buttons of his vest. But even in the absurdity of his dress, he had a certain carriage, a certain air that suggested he would be the last person in the room to feel uncomfortable about the way he looked. If there was a wave of disbelief that the "state fellow" had shown up at town meeting wearing a three-piece suit, there was also another wave of something very close to fear. It was not the suit that led to instant distrust, but the attitude of the wearer.

"In view of the lateness of the hour," Sorenson began, "I shall spare you formalities and move posthaste directly to the heart of the matter." He turned and with a grunt hoisted the map case to the table. He slid out a large multicolored map about four feet square and put it on the tripod.

"Why don't you cut the routine," Moose called out, "and get on with what it's going to cost us?"

Sorenson paused for just an instant in front of the map, then turned around. For a moment he stood as though he were thinking about something, and then slowly he said, "If you are concerned about an assessment for the repairs to Route Ten, you needn't be. No assessment has been planned."

For a moment there was dead silence in the hall while the people seemed to listen again to what Sorenson had just said. Then suddenly they understood, and there was loud applause and some shouting. Moose hollered, "You're all right, there, fella," and Hal Bitterley called out, "Splendid, splendid."

Sorenson looked at the people with a mixture of disbelief and amusement, and it occurred to him for an instant that it was like dealing with a group of schoolchildren. Their faces, eager and a little stupid-looking, radiated up at him as though he were some benevolent clown. He turned back to the tripod and said, "May I draw your attention to this topographical map?" He cleared his throat in a planned sort of way, as though it were a part of his whole speech, and then went on. "Oldenfield has for some time now been under study by governments at both the state and federal levels. Your position in the northern quadrant of the state is unique. The town lies in the geometric center of the only valley whose elevation is sufficient to sustain the passage of Interstate Eighty-eight-S, planned now for some three and a half years."

He turned full away from the map and faced the people squarely. There was no movement, no breath anywhere in the place, and for just a second Sorenson was confused.

"The evidence on this topographical map is indisputable," he said, as if arguing with someone who could not hear him. Even after a few more seconds there was no response, and finally he backed to the map and held up his right hand. "You see," he said, "the interstate is coming through here." He ran his hand down the center of the map to spell it out.

"Where you planning on putting it?" Bitterley shouted.

"Ain't nobody in this town needs an interstate," Calvin Runners hollered. He looked about for approval and support.

A great and general relief ran through the hall, almost a second wave of delight that there would be no assessment on the town. Quickly it gave way to defiance. "We need us that road fixed up," Runners called.

"You got any idea what getting to Newfield's like?" Moose shouted.

Finally Simmer raised his hand slightly from the table, and the remarks stopped instantly. Throughout all that had gone on, he had been sitting quietly at the table. Now, in genuine bewilderment, he shook his head slowly and then looked at Sorenson for a very long time. "Now you're saying that an interstate highway is going to come through this valley?" he finally asked. His confusion was plain on his face.

"It's hardly a suggestion," Sorenson said, almost delighted that finally he had someone to argue with. "It is a decision that has been made after due and proper study by the Department of Highways."

"Damn it, man, this valley's not more than three-quarters of a mile wide."

"Indeed, it is only three thousand two hundred feet wide," Sorenson answered in a low and even tone.

"Well, there ain't no room," Moose shouted, "not unless you're figuring to put it on stilts." A low wave of laughter swept the room, and Moose sat back in his chair with great satisfaction.

"Elevation will be required in certain sections," Sorenson said. Then quite suddenly there was silence in the hall, and Sorenson seized the opportunity. "There will, of course, be just and proper compensation."

"For *what?*" Simmer asked, his anger rising in his neck and face.

"For the houses," Sorenson answered.

With that he reached behind the map and flipped up a heavy plastic overlay that had two huge red stripes running vertically on it. He held it poised for just a moment, and then he said, "This, you see, is the right-of-way." Then he let it drop, and the two red lines blotted out the town completely. Suddenly there were a couple of pure, horrible gasps, followed by one distinct and very ugly groan. Then several audible "No's" followed, and finally there rose above all else, "Oh, please God in heaven."

What followed was a sickening confusion. People pivoted and squirmed in their seats as they sought from one another some meaning to what they had just heard. There was in the hall a feeling that they had observed a hideous accident and that collectively they were helpless to make things right. In frustration more than in anger at what Sorenson had told them, they began to call out to him.

"Where do you get off?" Millie Barnhope called in a strong voice from the back of the crowd.

"Hey, God almighty!" came from someone close to Millie.

"Take a ride, Buster!" Calvin Runners yelled.

"You heard Cal!" Moose shouted. "On your way. Go on—Concord's down that way."

"Nobody asked you, you know," someone else called.

The shouts were angry ones, moblike and threatening, but there was a feeling that somehow the people shouting were all in some invisible cage, that they were held to their seats by great unseen weights. For a moment Sorenson was shaken by the outbursts, but then it was as if he too realized that there was no threat to him. He raised his hand like a patient schoolteacher and stood relaxed. He began to talk before the calling out stopped. "First of all, it would be to your benefit to realize that these things take a great deal of time. And secondly, I will tell you in no uncertain terms that each and every one of you will benefit in this matter. The state has never cheated anyone in matters of this nature, and she never intends to."

"Just who the hell do you think you are?" came from the crowd.

Sorenson ignored the remark and went on, "It is my experience that rational discussion is the most civilized path to equitable determinations. I shall be in communication with your representatives here"—in a sweeping gesture he indicated Simmer and Culver—"to establish a series of meetings so that rational decisions may properly be reached."

Then, with a suddenness that was almost supernatural, Sorenson was gone. The tripod, the maps, the huge case, all in what seemed a flash were gone down the center aisle, and there was nothing to suggest that he had ever been there except the dull echo of the banging door. When even that was gone, the people turned in unison toward the small stage and stared at Simmer and Culver as though they held the secret to life. Simmer sat at the table with his hands folded, his body bent forward as if in prayer. Culver had long since sunk into a wooden chair just behind where Sorenson's map and tripod had been. Simmer raised a hand to call for quiet, but there was no sound anywhere in the hall. Finally, he said in a soft and firm voice, "Two hundred and twelve years we've been here. Nobody needs to say anything more than that."

"That's it, Carl," Bitterley called.

Simmer raised his finger and pointed it at the crowd as though he were talking directly to Sorenson. "They have yet to make the man who can shove around the town of Oldenfield, New Hampshire."

"He wants a fight," Moose called out, "he'll get it, all right."

Then quite suddenly there was a black silence in the hall, and no one moved; no one even really saw anything. There were only private stares, ghostlike, full of waste. Singly, soon in pairs, the people began to put on their wraps and move in silence toward the back of the hall. When they were outside, there rose the low hum of conversations, and from where they sat on the stage Simmer and Culver could hear an occasional "Hell, no," and "There ain't no way." Without even so much as a glance at Simmer, Culver left the stage and followed the last person out the door. Simmer watched him go, watched the door close and bang, and for a long time after the hall was empty he did not move.

Ellen Thomas was talking to Mr. Barker just outside the door of town hall when Culver came out. In the hard spotlight that flooded the whole entrance way and walk they looked to Culver like shrunken idols. Their faces looked too white to sustain life, and the spotlight fell on them in such a way that all around seemed an eternal blackness. Culver moved to them and stood a step away while they finished what they were saying. He heard Mr. Barker say, "Sequence of selection is only effective if the more emotional hymns are not used. Think always thematically."

Ellen suggested several hymns by page number, and as Mr. Barker was considering them, Culver stepped closer and quietly said, "For Christ's sake."

"With the help of Ellen I'm already planning a service for Sunday that I hope will comfort."

"I think I've got the perfect sequence of hymns," Ellen said. "What do you think of these?" But before she could say anything more Culver took her elbow and said, "Fine, fine."

As they walked down the narrow path that led away from town hall, Culver watched the other townspeople, the widows and widowers alone, disperse into the night. The street lights of the town stretched away only thirty yards in either direction, and as the people walked under them they looked to Culver utterly dwarfed and defeated. And then Culver and Ellen moved off through the last narrow little cone of light.

All during the day the people had been inside town hall, and they had not noticed the weather shifting like some uneasy gray blanket. But as they walked, Culver noticed that there was not the usual bite in the air, and that the slush in the street had not yet frozen up for the night. Then, as though miles off in the distance, there was the insistent rustling of the bare tree branches, stirring themselves, almost stretching, and Culver knew instinctively that the bark on the branches would be warm tonight. They would feel themselves, yawning and sensuous, the first night in five months they had not had their juices frozen back into their centers. The wind coming, rising, was from the southwest, billowy, almost a wind at ease with itself. It was coming like an answer to a question not yet asked, slipping the valleys, rolling with the sides of the mountains, shaping itself to everything in its way. It was a dry wind wetting itself with the snow still left in the pastures and fields, and when the first warm touch of it bumped against them, they both stiffened, but then almost immediately relaxed, and then bent themselves a little, like small sails balanced perfectly. "It's from the south, isn't it?" Ellen said.

"South, southwest," Culver answered. "Ought to blow three, four days."

"Then maybe spring," she said. "Maybe an early spring this year."

"Hardly likely," Culver said. He hooked his arm through Ellen's and gently tried to pull her close to him, but she did not seem to notice his gesture.

"You must always think affirmatively," Ellen said. "You know that."

"About what?"

"Spring," she answered. "All the good things of our world."

"Aren't you afraid?" Culver asked.

"Of that silly man? Of what's supposed to happen? Goodness, no," she said. They walked on in silence, and finally she told him, "You'll see. Spring'll be early."

As Culver's feet punched out wet holes in the soft slush, he realized that spring probably would be quite early that year. He could almost sense the earth under the snow cover beginning to shift itself, to start its first sad exertions, the slow cold boiling that would finally show itself in an oozy mud.

All the time Simmer sat alone on the stage, he was like a fierce motor revving ever higher. Although his face stayed blank, almost deathlike, his chest heaved, and the air he sucked in he quickly expelled, like a machine priming itself for some great effort. All the while in his mind he was watching Sorenson drive around Prior Lake on Route 10. He knew Sorenson was going slowly because of the chuckholes, and he also knew that he had plenty of time before Sorenson got to the far end of the lake where the road bent back toward Oldenfield. He measured his time almost by his heartbeats, and when he moved quickly from the stage he knew that if he took the logging road he would cut Sorenson off precisely where Route 10 split into two minor county roads.

When he got to his pickup truck, he immediately turned on the motor, but then instead of pulling off right away, he took a few seconds to check the plowing lights, two large white eyes that sat high in the truck's forehead. Then he pulled out the hydraulic lever that snapped the seven-foot plow from the ground and brought it snugly into place in front of the grille. For just a second or two Simmer felt the weight of the plow bend the truck forward and down. Next, Simmer slowly shifted the truck into four-wheel drive, and then all of the vehicle's power seemed to organize itself to move quietly through his own body.

When he drove onto the logging road, the truck was not even slowed by the foot of snow. In fact, it seemed more at ease going through the virgin snow than if it had been made to go over the half-decayed asphalt on Route 10. As he drove, Simmer knew that he would easily be in time to cut off Sorenson, but as he neared the downward part of the road that led to Route 10, he saw where the snow had drifted across the logging road and made a barrier nearly five feet high. And he knew it was not powder snow that he was going to hit. He knew all too well that stitched throughout the drift were layers of ice that marked the depth of each storm that winter. He just had time to glance at the height of the plow, and its alignment reassured him. Then suddenly he hit the drift. There was a dull thud, like a severe body blow, and a dry splash of white and silver debris spread in a kind of slow motion around the hood of the truck and then in a flash struck the windshield. Simmer never even flinched, and the truck, as though a perfect extension of him, kept moving on as if the drift had been some misplaced cloud.

The truck hummed along, almost more powerful than Simmer had ever felt it, and when he saw the lake from the top of a small rise, he slowed the truck and then stopped it just a few feet from where the logging road met Route 10. He turned off the lights, and as he sat in the cab he could feel the gentle vibrations of the motor blend with the darkness.

When he turned off the engine, just for a moment nothing moved; no sound; only the quiet frosty blinking of the stars over the lake, and Simmer's own breath that came steadily in small gray billows from his open mouth. For a moment he was terribly confused and then very angry. He looked up Route 10 for several long seconds, searching for Sorenson's taillights, and just as he was about to conclude that he had missed him, he turned the other way and saw that indeed he had not.

Slowly picking his way around the chuckholes, Sorenson was coming at a speed which clearly showed that the road terrified him. The headlights of the Chevrolet bobbed and weaved like some mysterious drunken animal as Sorenson gradually approached. He went by at no more than fifteen miles an hour, and when he was just past the logging road, Simmer methodically reached for the ignition key and slowly turned it. He pulled back on the hydraulic lever, and the plow rose from the ground and poised itself again in front of the grille. Then Simmer pushed in the other lever, and the plow swung sharply to the left. Immediately he pulled hard on the same lever, and the plow swung far to the right, as though of itself it would follow Sorenson's car. Then Simmer straightened the plow and eased the truck onto the road.

Sorenson was no more than fifty yards ahead, and Simmer approached quickly, his lights off, his left hand poised just above the plow levers. His plan was to run Sorenson off the road, to put him into or over one of the four-foot snowbanks that followed the sides of the road like two huge rolled blankets.

At the first bump of the plow against the rear door of the station wagon, Sorenson was off like a jackrabbit, leaving Simmer fumbling in first gear as he sped ahead for thirty or forty yards. But it was then that he began to fishtail, and only the jolts the car took from hitting the chuckholes kept him on the road. Simmer watched for Sorenson to spin out, and when he did not, Simmer cursed and accelerated quickly toward the weaving car. This time there was no bump; there was a crunching, cutting sound, and the rear door on the Chevrolet folded like cardboard.

"Good, you bastard," Simmer mumbled, his face suddenly a twisted, hideous thing. He hit the back of the car again and again, and it was clear that his plan to put Sorenson over the snowbank had been momentarily forgotten.

Sorenson held the Chevrolet's wheel with increasingly steady hands, almost as though he knew that in a few more seconds he would again bring things under his own control.

For the next quarter of a mile Simmer almost joyfully banged the rear of Sorenson's car in hard, rhythmic jolts. But the pleasure he got out of it was his first mistake. He misjudged the distance to the last fork in the road, and when he realized it, he tried desperately to accelerate to correct for his error. But the powerful burst from the pickup came too late; it sent both vehicles through the snowbank dead ahead. They careened through the snow,

Sorenson's car clearly out of control and headed for the lake. Simmer was able to stop the truck about halfway to the lake—just in time to see Sorenson's car hit the ice and then, like some strange supernatural boat, sail out onto it in a long, lazy spin. It came to a stop with its headlights pointing straight ahead, and for an instant it looked to Simmer as though absolutely nothing had happened. He eased the truck into first gear, adjusted the plow a little higher, and, like a hunter going in to finish his kill, he drove onto the ice.

That was his second mistake. On the ice the vehicles were equal. Simmer's four-wheel drive no longer gave him the advantage, and when he hit the side of Sorenson's car head-on, it shot away from him with almost no damage. In frustration he accelerated, but all four of his wheels spun futilely, the truck motionless like some huge paralyzed animal. Then in fierce anger he pushed the accelerator almost to the floor. The spinning of the wheels made the truck do a small dance on the ice as it moved first to the left and then slowly back to the right. Simmer hit both sets of headlights, the regular truck lights and the powerful plowing lights. Together they shone brilliantly on the driver's side of the station wagon, and Simmer was suddenly horrified to see that Sorenson's head was tipped back against the edge of the seat and that he was laughing as hard as any sane man could.

Simmer let the motor die off to a steady idle, and then with his foot just barely touching the accelerator he eased the truck past the rear of Sorenson's car and on toward the edge of the lake. He went up the way he had come down and then turned back onto Route 10 and was gone. When he had seen Sorenson's laughing face, it had ruined some delicate fiber deep inside him; something had seemed to snap and wither all in a brief instant, and as he drove back toward Oldenfield, he felt an immense fatigue roll through his whole body.

Millie Barnhope and Moose Krause walked away from town hall without a word between them. Jerky hobbled along behind them on his crutches. As they moved off toward the store, Moose looked up for a moment at the post office silhouetted against the black sky and the scrambling gray clouds. There was an instant when the building looked to him like an enormous head bent in sadness, but then quickly he looked away and off into the distance. As he walked he kicked at the sparkling little mounds of slush. Next to him Millie walked on as if she could go through a building. Her shoulders were squared off, her fists clenched; her jaw was set into a hard, solid line. Every few steps, her lips curled and parted as she swore silently to herself.

"Well, Jesus," Moose finally said to the night.

"What gets me is his *gall,*" Millie said as though to release all of her feelings on that one word. She was silent for several more steps, and then she said, "Who the hell says he's God? Never even so much as seen him before, and he's standing in front of everybody saying, 'There will be compensation.' " She let her voice rise in singsong fashion as she mocked Sorenson. "If I could get my hands on him," she went on in her own voice, "I swear to God I'd kill him."

Then again she fell silent, and suddenly the night around her seemed a bleak and endless thing. She took no notice of the gentle wind that bumped against the back of her short brown hair. Her whole life seemed to her then as worthless as a thimbleful of black ink, and she felt as though she had been turned into a vacuum, suddenly sucking up nothing but anger and blind rage. It was clear from the expression on her face that if she could have gotten her hands on Sorenson, certainly she would have tried to kill him, tried mightily to erase him from her life as fast as she could. "It was his way of saying everything," she went on suddenly, "his attitude. Like he was God almighty."

"Him with that suit," Moose said.

Neither really heard the other, and as they passed out of the small white cone of the last street light they did not speak. The only light visible was way in the distance, the thin sharp needle point of light in front of Millie's store. And a couple of stars riding high over the clouds.

When they went into the store, Millie put two chunks of wood into the Franklin stove. She stepped back from it and for a few moments watched the chunks begin to sputter and crackle; then tiny flames searched the corners of the wood and shot up. She kicked the door of the stove with her foot, spinning it shut with a soft click. As she took off her coat she watched Moose put a six-pack on the counter and rip down the side. He popped a can and drank about half of it. "Oh, that's better, that's better," he said. He handed a can to Jerky, who held it unopened for a moment and then set it back on the counter. Millie came around the back of the counter, and as she got to the small cash register she seemed to falter slightly, as if at that moment Sorenson's news had reached her again. "Oh, my Christ," she said, bending her head and upper body as though she had just been hit hard in the belly.

Moose opened another can of beer and began to drink it as eagerly as the first. He held the can well above his head, and his mouth moved over the top of it with the motions of a baby sucking milk. He drank hard from the can, and when he stopped for breath he kept the can raised above his head, the thin little opening pressed tightly against his lips, as his nostrils flared for air. Millie and Jerky watched him drink, and then Millie said, "Slow the hell down, will you?"

"Let him be," Jerky said.

"Oh, *yes*," Moose said as he took the can from his mouth. A small curl of white foam ran from the corner of his mouth and then disappeared as it seemed to be absorbed into his skin. "Now it's the second one that's heaven," he said, as though beginning a long lecture. But no one heard him, and he quickly looked away.

Then after a second or two the silence was on them all again, a fixed, private staring that descended like an instantly transmittable virus. Their eyes got slightly larger in their heads; their bodies were caught and frozen by some poisonous air. They stood that way, each looking beyond the others, beyond the boundaries of the store and even the town, and for just the barest instant it seemed that never again would they move. It was Millie who spoke first. "He . . ." she began, but for a moment she could not even remember Sorenson's name. "He said it'd take a long time."

"It could be a couple of years," Moose said. "Christ, maybe longer." He rolled the empty beer can in his hands, absently reading the label on both sides.

"I was thinking maybe they'd be coming tomorrow," Millie said with a vague, stupid smile.

There was another long moment in which the moody silence seemed to be staging a comeback, but then Moose broke in and said, "You know what the post office is worth?" Neither Millie nor Jerky looked at him. "If I was in a selling mood I could get me twenty-eight, thirty thousand for it. With the half acre in back," he added.

"The guy's officer material," Jerky said to his mother.

Millie turned full toward him and stood looking at him for a long time. "What can we do?" she said. The look on her face was one of ultimate and final despair; she did not really expect an answer to her question.

"First, delay them," Jerky answered quickly. "Fight them here, right now, before they get a foothold. Then we fight them in court, and if we have to, we can fight them out there." He raised his arm and pointed toward the door and toward the fields and woods far beyond the town. Then, as though he had suddenly remembered an urgent errand, he propped himself on his crutches and moved like some giant toy toward the back of the store.

"Where are you going?" Millie asked.

"To clean my weapon, sir."

The Reverend Mr. Barker

Barker hated Oldenfield for several reasons, not the least of which was his having been assigned there nearly nineteen years before. It had been understood then that the assignment was temporary, that as soon as the old minister in Newfield died, Barker would get that job. And for all of his ministry Barker had dearly wanted that church. It was one of the most beautiful in all New England, a great wooden structure with a rich and stunning interior. Running the Baptist church in Newfield was very much like running a small and highly profitable business, and the minister there was, by definition, one of the influential people in the whole area. But the old minister had held on, even gotten better it seemed, and for many years now it was as if Barker had simply been forgotten.

But it had not been all bleak for Barker. During the years, he had had his moments in the Newfield church. He'd held services the four Sundays in August when the old minister was on vacation, and he had been called to substitute numerous times when the old man was ill. By no means, though, did Barker confine himself to visiting the Newfield church only on those days he preached. Every time he went to the town he drove past the church, once coming, once going; and occasionally he stopped the car by the side of the road and looked at it for a long time. He loved its lines, its elegance, everything about it. Always when he stopped by the church he saw himself in the small pulpit preaching his heart out.

But the years had dragged on for Barker, and as he turned fifty-five he began to wonder if the call to New-field would ever come. His bitterness at having to stay in

Oldenfield was certainly not without justification. It was a hard church in a hard town. There was very little money for the church there, and Barker had to do many of the chores that in a larger and wealthier town would have been done by the sexton. He did all of the maintenance: he painted the church annually, cleaned it weekly, mowed the lawns in the summer, shoveled the walks in the winter. Simmer plowed the snow from the long circular driveway, but except for that, he had no help. And the house that came with the church was a wreck. There were cracks everywhere and floorboards that sagged hopelessly, and the insulation was so inadequate that often on winter mornings Barker could see his breath as it mingled with his steaming tea.

The only person who had sustained him through most of his years in Oldenfield was Ellen Thomas, and certainly she was the only person who knew of his ambition. He had suddenly blurted it out one fine Easter morning six years before. There had been an ice storm the night before, but the morning had broken fresh and bright, the trees coated and tingling as if they had been made in a crystal factory. But only nine people were sitting in the church when Ellen came back to tell him it was time to start. He had looked at her, his eyes wild and sad all at the same time. "I never did anything in my life to deserve this," he said. "I am better than this church, this town. I have a larger destiny." Then he turned from her and said, "Have you heard my sermons in Newfield? They are grand things; they are inspired by the people there, by the very building itself. What am I doing in *this?*" He spread his arms in bewilderment. "I am right for that place—do you understand me?"

She looked at him with genuine compassion, and then she reminded him of the advice he had given her when her son had been killed: "We are not meant to understand God's will."

When Barker got back to his house, Mrs. Keller was waiting for him. She was sitting in her 1954 Chevrolet, the motor running smoothly, the lights soft white outlines against the black. As he came up the long drive in front of the church, the lights caught him squarely, and he squinted and dropped his head against them. When he came around the side of the car he saw that the window was already rolled down. As he leaned over, Mrs. Keller said, "He's gone."

"Was it easy?"

"Hardly."

"Come into the house. We'll have some tea."

"He had a vision just at the end," Mrs. Keller said. She had not yet looked at Barker. "He thought"—she started to go on, then dropped her head—"dear God, he thought he was at Sears in Manchester. And everybody he ever knew in his life was there."

"Come into the house," Barker said again. "We'll have some tea and I'll call Mr. Bitterley directly." He opened the car door for her.

"And Mr. James," Mrs. Keller said. "See if he can dig the grave now. Maybe the ground is thawed enough. I couldn't bear it if he had to go in the ice house and just lie there a month."

"We'll all do our best." Barker led her up the steps, and as they got to the front door he said, "Is there anyone with him now?"

"His dog."

An hour later only Jerky had left the group in Millie's store, and he had just gone to the back to smoke a joint. Simmer had come in a few minutes after Jerky left, and now he stood with an unopened beer can and looked vacantly at the stove. Millie and Moose seemed to be looking directly at each other, but neither saw the other. Moose was propped against one of the six-by-six roof supports, and Millie sat in a cheap lawn chair just behind the cash register. Simmer rolled the beer can in his hands as if it were a warm bubble. Collectively they looked like discards from some giant puppet show.

It was a full second or two before anyone realized that Hal Bitterley had come into the store. "Beer?" Millie said to him as she came out of her chair and swept a can from the counter.

"Maybe on the way back if you're still open," he told her. "All I'll take now is some Pepto-Bismol." He gestured with his head behind Millie, and she turned and took it from the rack above her head. "Old man Keller's gone," Bitterley announced to the room.

"Ain't no great loss," Moose said.

"You going up there now?" Simmer asked.

"Going to Newfield with him," Bitterley said. "Mrs. Keller said he ain't to go in the ice house. No, sir, under no circumstances."

"Hospital there'll keep him only a day or two," Simmer told him.

"Grave's got to be dug right away, she said. Like yesterday, don't you know."

"Ground's not thawed down but two, three inches," Simmer said.

"She said she don't care. He's got to go in the ground."

"Hell of a lot easier going through concrete," Moose put in.

"That'll be Bony James's problem," Bitterley said. He slowly unscrewed the cap from the bottle and took a long drink from it. When he took the bottle away from his mouth, his lips were pink and slippery from the liquid. He wiped his mouth and said, "That state fellow's set my gut on fire." He took another long swallow and said, "The son of a bitch. Mrs. Bitterley's to home already going through all her papers. She's about gone crazy."

"Tell her not to worry," Simmer said.

48

"And you tell the wind it's not to blow," Bitterley threw at him. "I'm not halfway home and she's gone all to pieces." It was clear that he was angrier at his wife than at Sorenson. "She says she can't ever live nowheres else."

"There's not one of us that could," Simmer said.

"I could go with my children," Moose said.

"Shut up," Millie told him.

"Whole place, even with the land, wouldn't bring but fourteen thousand," Bitterley said. He paused a second, then added, "If that."

"There'll be no selling of houses and land," Simmer said, and there was something in his voice that made the others turn and look closely at him. He was looking beyond them to some indefinite place. "You tell Mrs. Bitterley I said that."

"Sure," Bitterley said. He looked at Simmer as if suddenly he were afraid of him. "I got to get me on to Newfield," he said quickly. He put the Pepto-Bismol into his back pocket and left.

Millie and Moose kept their eyes on Simmer as if they expected him to continue with a complete and satisfying answer to all of their problems. But he said nothing more, and the only sound in the whole place was the quiet spitting of the wood chunks in the stove. Even in the silence no one heard Jerky come out of the back of the store and stand like a small fragile statue, his eyes great vacant discs.

The cemetery was at the opposite end of the town from Simmer's Garage. It sat on a pretty knoll just off Route 10, and a good number of gravesites faced the road. They also faced the setting sun, and on warm summer evenings the headstones cast huge shadows that stretched up the knoll for many yards. In the winter the shadows lay across the snow like carefully spread long rows of soot. In the early morning the cemetery was a cold dark place, the sun completely blocked by the giant pine trees at the top of the knoll. But the striking thing about the whole place was how old it looked. There was a wasted, used-up quality to it, and a certain uneasy impression that far more people had been buried there than the number of headstones indicated. Roots were everywhere. They rose out of the ground like arms and sank back in little curling waves. Sprinkled about in places where the snow had begun to draw back were layers of pine needles and swatches of leaves in various stages of decay. They seemed to make a permanent soundproof carpet for the whole place.

The next morning, when Bony James came to dig Mr. Keller's grave, there was barely any light in the sky. Off to the east were long lines of needle-shaped clouds, white like spilled lotion. As the sun began to rise, the clouds changed to a light blood color for a few moments, and then, when the sun was finally past them, their undersides turned a dullish black. Bony walked up the small graveled road that ran between the two largest pines on top of the knoll. He stood for a moment and looked down at the graves. In front of him was recorded the whole modern history of Oldenfield. He looked at the places where he had dug nine and ten graves in the same close family area, and then at others where one headstone staked its own solitary plot.

Bony was a tall, thin man in his late sixties, and there was about him the sense of great strength slowly seeping from his body. He walked in a way that suggested he had once been enormously strong; the pickax and shovel he carried were held like toys.

He left the narrow road and swept down the knoll in long sure strides. His heels dug into the soft juicy turf under the snow like the little crescents of horseshoes. Near the bottom he turned and walked the four short steps to the Keller plot, which he had laid out almost twenty years before. It was a small rectangular area with barely enough space for two graves. Mr. Keller was to be on the right. When Bony dropped his shovel into the thin snow cover, it made no sound. For a moment he looked down at the area where he would dig, and with his eyes he drew the outline for the grave.

The first blow of the pickax buried the head deep in the snow, and when Bony pulled it up in a sure, easy motion a chunk of hard brown dirt flipped over and lay mixed with the snow. He worked steadily along an even line near the foot of the grave, each blow bringing up another clod of dirt the size of a worn old shoe. The line Bony followed was as straight as if he had set a string, and he went methodically around the whole outline of the grave. With each thrust of the pickax the area of snow on top of the gravesite grew smaller. Finally, when he had removed the top layer of soil to a depth of four inches, he knew that the job would take at least three days. Under the top level of snow, just as Moose Krause had said, the ground was as hard as concrete. The grave looked as though a blanket had been removed to reveal a brown, stone coffin already in place. In an angry way Bony swung the pickax as hard as he could, but the only result all his strength achieved was a small frozen chip of dirt that flew up and bumped against his chest.

An hour and a half later, around eight o'clock, Bony was not much farther into the grave. Next to him was a pile of dirt chips and flakes of frozen soil, and although the pickax only bounced off the ground, Bony swung it in a smooth, steady rhythm. Occasionally he would strike the ground just right and a chunk of dirt as hard as a jewel would fling itself into the air as though it had just come alive.

It was Bony who heard the trucks first, like the distant grumblings of a thunderstorm pounding Newfield. At first he paid the sound no mind at all; it seemed to mix with the clink of the pickax chewing at the ground. When the noise rose above Bony's efforts, he stopped and turned. From far up Route 10 the first group were coming like the remnants of a lost army. They moved down the road slowly, picking their way among the chuckholes, and after a few more minutes Bony saw that leading them all was a Chevrolet station wagon with two red flags rising from its front bumper. On the front doors was the state seal surrounded by DEPARTMENT OF HIGHWAYS. Bony stood still and watched as the trucks passed him: he counted eighteen ten-wheelers, all filled with great mounds of gravel and crushed stone; behind them were three graders, two bucket loaders, and, still farther on, two flatbed trucks with bulldozers secured to their middles with huge chains. Behind them were three backhoes, and one giant flatbed truck stacked high with culverts.

The trucks went all the way down to Simmer's Garage, where the last of the serious chuckholes were, and then stopped and dumped their loads into three enormous piles. Quickly the bucketloaders began to take large bites of gravel and stone, whirl around, nose themselves toward the chuckholes, and dump their contents smoothly. Then the bulldozers moved in to flatten and pack, and finally the graders rotated and adjusted their blades and began to go over the whole road surface.

All the while Simmer stood between his two Shell pumps and watched. His gaze alternated between the machinery and Sorenson, who sat in the station wagon and stared straight back at him.

It was not long before Culver drove down the side of the road at a dangerously fast clip. Twice he had to brake hard to avoid a backing bulldozer. When he finally pulled into Simmer's, he was yelling even before he got the window down: "From the post office it sounds like all hell's breaking loose."

"I imagine it's about to," Simmer said, nodding across the way to where Sorenson still sat.

Culver got out of his pickup and stood beside Simmer next to the pumps. He watched the heavy machinery groan away at its task, and then he fastened his gaze on Sorenson. Immediately he saw Sorenson give him a slight nod. "Did you talk to the bastard?" Culver asked.

Simmer turned and looked out over the road as though he were watching a child playing with toy machinery. Then he shook his head slowly.

"Why not?" Culver asked.

"You sleep last night?"

"Course I slept last night," Culver said.

"Good," Simmer said. "Then you talk to him."

Sorenson beat them both to it. He slowly got out of his car and walked toward them. As he approached, a bulldozer rumbled past him, and he had to stop for it. As he stood frozen to his spot in the middle of the road, his body shook with the vibrations from the huge machine. Finally, when he was close to the gas pumps, he said, "Good morning, gentlemen."

"Go to hell," Simmer quietly said and looked away.

The reply hit Sorenson like a quick little jab in the face. He tried to shake it off, to smile a little, but he could not.

"What are you doing here?" Culver asked.

Sorenson moved his eyes from Simmer to Culver as he said, "You will never see a more profound demonstration of good will."

"Fix the goddamn road and get out of here," Simmer told him.

This time Sorenson reacted as if he'd gotten a kidney punch, and he was suddenly on fire with rage. "Don't ever speak to me that way," he said. "Not *ever.*" Just when it seemed he would go further out of control, his anger subsided and he said in a calm voice, "We have to talk, you know. We have to have a meeting."

"You know we're going to take it to court," Culver

said. He smiled in a most satisfied way and looked to Simmer.

"Yes, yes, of course you are," Sorenson said. "And you might get an extra month out of it, maybe even six weeks." He seemed genuinely bored by the conversation. "But really you ought to save your money."

"We'll win," Culver said, as if to reassure himself.

"Don't be silly," Sorenson said. "Part of my job is to pick a town that can't win in court."

"And why won't we win?" Culver asked.

"Population decline," Sorenson answered. "A simple census graph and extrapolation. In thirty, perhaps thirty-five years Oldenfield won't exist anyway."

Both Culver and Simmer were for the moment stunned by Sorenson. Clearly, they were shaken by Sorenson's information, but what seemed to carry more power than that was the way he delivered it. He was full of statistics, brimming with facts, bubbling over with a confidence and power that even he seemed unaware of. His manner implied that he was not just one man but a militia of people drawn together to create a power somehow greater than the sum of all its parts.

Just as Sorenson was about to press Culver and Simmer for a meeting time, Bony James's truck snaked its way around a road grader and came to a stop next to them. "Mr. Simmer," Bony said from the truck, "I need the jackhammer."

"Hoses are all rotted out," Simmer told him without really looking at him.

"Then Mr. Keller gets to lie on top," Bony said. "Nobody's going down another inch without a jack."

"I've got some dynamite," Culver said.

"Worth a try," Bony answered.

As if they mutually understood, Culver got into his truck, and Bony started off behind him.

"What's the problem?" Sorenson asked Simmer.

"Digging a grave in frozen ground," Simmer answered. He looked at Sorenson with utter hate.

"I could let you have a jackhammer and a backhoe."

"Nobody's begging you."

"I know that."

After a moment in which it seemed the two men were trying to stare each other down, Simmer finally said, "All right, then," and they turned and went to Sorenson's station wagon.

As they got in, Sorenson said, "I knew it was you last night."

Looking directly at him, Simmer said, "Good for you."

Bony was digging a small hole for the dynamite when Culver came over the top of the knoll, carrying the dynamite in a small brown sack. At the grave he set it carefully where the headstone would finally go. When the hole was deep enough, the two men carefully packed the dynamite to achieve as much downward thrust as possible. They detonated it from behind two large headstones twenty-five yards away. The sound made was a high-pitched one, like fifty rifles all going off at once on a clear autumn morning, and some pieces of frozen dirt showered down on them. But the effort was a complete failure. Instead of a hole nearly four feet deep, which would have been the result had the ground been thawed, they saw only a concave area no more than a foot across and less than six inches deep. "Three tons of dynamite wouldn't probably dent it," Bony said.

At that moment Sorenson and Simmer came over the top of the knoll in the station wagon. Hooked to the ball on the back of the wagon was the compressor for the jackhammer. Sorenson eased the car down the narrow graveled road and past the grave. Then he swung it off the road and over two graves, backing it carefully so that the compressor's wheels were just at the edge of Mr. Keller's plot.

Behind the station wagon came the backhoe, its giant claw poised close to its body like a proud deformed arm. Sorenson was out of the car quickly, waving the backhoe to its position just above the grave. Then, with Culver and Bony helping him, he took the jackhammer out of the back of the car and began to attach the hoses. When he had finished, he started the compressor and immediately put the jackhammer to the frozen ground. He handled the heavy awkward instrument with great ease, and Culver and Bony stood to one side as he guided the blade into the ground in a series of rude, biting thrusts.

"She'll do the job," Bony shouted to Culver above the noise.

Sorenson lifted the jackhammer out of the four-inch hole and waved the backhoe into motion. The long yellow arm flexed itself and then moved slowly out and away from its body. From a height of six or seven feet the claw dropped to the frozen ground at the foot of the grave. Its teeth dug in for just an instant and then began to slip across the top of the dirt in long shiny scars. The claw came up at the head of the grave as empty as it had begun. Sorenson motioned the backhoe operator to try a second time to rake the grave, but as the claw started upward he thought better of it and waved it off. He stepped onto the grave itself and examined the ground and the marks made by the claw. Shaking his head, he turned to Culver and Bony. "The jack's the only way you'll get in," he said.

As though following orders, Bony picked up the jackhammer and dragged it onto the grave top. He began at once to lean on it, pushing it as hard as he could, while the sound of the compressor rose high over the cemetery and drowned out the bulldozers, trucks and graders far down Route 10.

Sorenson watched Bony's efforts for only a few seconds; then he turned to Simmer. Above the din from the compressor he shouted, "Why I'm here is to set a meeting time." When Simmer ignored him, Sorenson said, "There must be a time set. There must be organization." He sounded as if he had just consulted some huge mental timetable and was well behind schedule.

Simmer turned slowly toward him and said, "Go away. Just fix the road and go away."

"Can we talk in the car?"

"No."

"I'm going to tell you something, then," Sorenson said. He stepped directly in front of Simmer and took his full attention. "Don't make me be devious. Do you hear that?" Simmer nodded without looking at him. "You wouldn't like that."

"I won't meet with you, because there isn't anything to talk about," Simmer finally said. He turned a little so that he faced him directly. "You are not going to raze this town. You're not even going to lay a finger on one brick, not on one stick of lumber." There was fire in Simmer as he said it, and if the jackhammer had not been going he would have sounded insane.

Sorenson looked at him for a long moment, his eyes moving over Simmer's face. "You cannot *will* me away," he finally said to Simmer.

Then both men seemed simultaneously to realize that words were a foolish thing. Sorenson stepped back alongside of Simmer, and together they watched Bony thrust and shove at the frozen ground. They stood like that for a long time, Culver a little off to the side, and it seemed for an instant as if each thought the grave being dug was for him. Their faces were little knots of disbelief and anger, and they looked like sick people not quite fully aware of how sick they are. All except the backhoe operator, that is, who was just barely visible through the montage of reflections in the cab's windshield. He sat behind the controls with his chin on his chest, his arms folded, as he nodded in a light, peaceful sleep.

After a little time of constantly working the jackhammer, Bony had succeeded in turning the earth so that it looked very much like the top layer of a spring garden. Where there had been only rock-hard ground, there was now a kind of organization of chunks of frozen dirt which lay ankle-deep around Bony and the jackhammer. In places the ice crystals sparkled and shone as if from a precious mineral, but near the foot of the grave, where Bony had begun, the chunks were beginning to thaw quickly into a slick mud.

Stirred suddenly out of what seemed an intense private dream, Sorenson snapped his head away from the digging and toward his trucks and machinery far down Route 10. As he started for the station wagon he said to Simmer, "This is your last chance."

Simmer lifted one arm from across his chest and waved it in front of his face as if to dismiss a summer fly.

"Very well," Sorenson said. He got immediately into his car, turned it around very slowly on the small road, backed it carefully to the edge of one grave, and then cut the front wheels very sharply to avoid another. Turned and straight on the graveled road, Sorenson hit the accelerator. The thunder of the jackhammer covered the sound of the station wagon's leaving, but as it was driven away its rear wheels threw up little pebbles and fine gravel that showered Culver and Simmer and then spread evenly over the snow around them.

A few minutes later Bony paused, and the only sound in the whole cemetery came from some birds high in a huge old oak over near the middle plots. Finally, Culver looked at Simmer and said, "I'd best go tell Barker he'll have his service tomorrow." He looked to Bony, who nodded at him, and then dragged the jackhammer off the grave and set it in the snow. He picked up his long-handled shovel and began to move the chunks of dirt into a pile at one side of the grave.

Simmer and Culver stayed only a few more moments, then left together. That seemed somehow a signal that woke the backhoe operator, who immediately started his machine and followed Culver and Simmer up the road and over the knoll.

Bony worked on steadily all through the rest of the morning. Near eleven o'clock he was knee-deep in the grave, where he could feel the ground begin to give itself up more easily. By midafternoon the job was thoroughly under control, the ground four feet down soft and open to the pickax and shovel.

Three

A week later the trucks and bulldozers were gone from Route 10, and Sorenson had not been seen since his little tantrum in the cemetery. The road to Newfield had a slick new coating on it, covered with new sand, and all things were once more as they should be. Moose Krause again made his biweekly trip to the state liquor store in Newfield, The Reverend Mr. Barker had plenty of time to drive past the Newfield church, Simmer had a fresh gas delivery, Millie's business had picked up a little from the transients, and Culver was finally free of the complicated state request forms for spring maintenance. The helplessness and despair that had hit the town with Sorenson's news were gone. It was as though most of the people had thought they would find themselves pulled from their homes, their belongings dumped in the street, and the brand-new Interstate 88-S put down through their village overnight. When no such thing happened, and when the sounds of the heavy machinery were gone from the road, the people were able to dismiss the sickening fears of the first few nights. Instead of the tortured anxious rumors at the post office in the mornings, there was now a gentle return to more familiar conversations.

What helped most was the weather. It seemed that with Sorenson's news, there came an unconscious comfort from the weather. For the first time the winter sharpness was completely gone from the air; the nighttime temperatures did not fall below freezing for a time sufficient to stop or even slow up the genuine thaw that had set in. The mornings were lovely precious events that week, and the morning Mr. Keller was buried was a perfect one. There was no wind until around eleven o'clock, and the sun spread a liquid warmth all through the town. Little rivers of pure water ran freely from the three-foot snowbanks that wound through the town like giant ropes. Behind the snowbanks the lawns in front of the houses were beginning to free themselves, and the trees throughout the town seemed more flexible and full as the buds began to slide back from their new leaves. The afternoons, at least until the wind came up and brought in shovelfuls of clouds, were almost hot, and there was a half hour when anyone outside could feel the sun drill away at his back.

Talk about Sorenson and the interstate was replaced quickly by small intimate conversation about what a lovely service Barker had given for Mr. Keller. There was routine again, but it seemed to come back on the town with almost frightening speed. In another week it was not so much that Sorenson was out of their lives; there was a strange, almost supernatural feeling in the town that he had never existed at all.

The days and the weather rolled on with the gorgeous blooming quality of a true early spring. Three weeks later, by the end of April, the snow was down from the top fringes of the mountain, the run-off streams had bubbled up their banks and slid back into trickles, and the wind at night blew from the south-southwest in warm dark bundles. Gardens were sprouting all over town: the tomato plants were rigid in the ground, and cornstalks were already a foot high in some gardens; and in the town there was the feeling that all were involved in some wonderful forward thrust, that for the first time in five years the gardens and other early spring plantings would not be crippled or thoroughly wasted by a late snowstorm or a killer frost.

The post office was much more crowded than usual on the morning of April 30, a good number of the townspeople having left their box-rental payments until the last possible moment. There was a line of nine people waiting for Moose Krause when he opened up at seven o'clock, and throughout the morning they came in twos and threes to pay their rents. To every third person or so Moose was downright rude, saying things like, "You'd think some people would make some plans sometimes." Then quickly he would take the fifty cents and give out the little yellow receipt. He was about to close for lunch when Mrs. Keller came in holding up her arms as though she wanted to surrender to him. In one hand she held a fifty-cent piece, in the other a white index card. "I honestly don't know which end's which," she said. She gave Moose the things she held. He dropped the coin into the change drawer at his waist, then held the index card and studied it for a moment. "How long you going to be here?" he asked her.

"They've asked me to come and live with them," she said. "It's my niece's place down past Concord."

Moose picked up a pencil and scribbled in the zip code. "Who's looking after your house?" he asked.

"I sold it," she said.

"You just up and sold it?" he said. "I mean just like that?"

"Things aren't near the same with Mr. Keller gone," she said.

"I'll be damned." Neither of them was really talking to the other. Moose looked again at the card as though to check its information once more, and with his eyes down he asked, "Who'd you sell to?"

"A bachelor gentleman," she said. "A Mr. Sorenson from Concord."

The news hit the town in two waves. First there was the utter shock that Sorenson had actually bought out one of the townspeople, and following that there came sweeping through the town the anxiety of whom Sorenson would try to take next. The people were outraged at Mrs. Keller, and even though she had not been to town meeting and had not known who Sorenson was, there was talk of getting even with her for having sold out at a time when, as some put it, the town had to stand together at all costs. That very evening at Millie's store there was angry talk against Mrs. Keller, and Jerky Barnhope in a fit of self-righteousness suggested to the others that they go up to her house and cut the utility wires.

"Christ, boy, you make me sick," Simmer said to Jerky. "Mrs. Keller didn't have the faintest idea who the hell Sorenson was." He paused and then said, "He probably stole the house from her anyway."

"What do you think he paid for it?" Moose said. It was clear that the money was by far the most important thing on his mind.

"Assessment three years ago was nine thousand," Simmer answered.

"That'd make it near eighteen thousand on the open market." Moose's head was tilted back slightly as if he were trying to calculate many different figures all at once.

"I'll bet he didn't pay a cent more than fifteen," Millie said. She picked up a ruler next to the cash register and held it like a headless hammer. She tapped the counter a couple of times and then said, "A stupid old woman like that."

"It makes you want to get a gun," Jerky put in.

"You shut up," Millie told him.

"We're not going about this right," Simmer said di-

63

rectly to all of them. His great red face suddenly came alive. "The man came in here and told us open and aboveboard what he was going to do, and not a soul believed him." He looked as if he himself had suddenly understood only now what was happening to him and the town.

"He can't take the town," Moose said, a broad stupid smile across his mouth.

"Just because he got Keller's place sure don't mean he's going to get all the rest of us," Millie said.

Simmer looked at her, his face fresh and full of life for the first time in weeks. "But what you don't see is that the man has all the money," he said.

"All we got to do," Moose said, "is all stick right together and tell him no, down to every last one of us."

"You're getting dumber by the day," Simmer told him. "A man like Sorenson, he works on your greed. You wait."

"I'm telling you—" Moose started to say.

"There's not a person in this town ever known real money," Simmer said.

"I'm all right," Moose said.

"You're better off than most, what with your nineteen thousand," Simmer said, and he watched Moose's face curl in great surprise. "But that's not real money. It was, but not now, not no longer. Real money's what Sorenson's got. If he wanted, you know, he could come up here with the state's checkbook and buy this town out in one afternoon."

"Not if we all stick right together," Moose said.

"You ever had a chance at forty thousand cash?" Simmer asked.

There was a long silence in the store, the only sound the easy fire low in the Franklin stove. After a while Simmer said, "It's plain, you see, plain as the nose on your face. We're going to lose." He turned and left the store as if he had just come in and found no one there.

After Simmer was gone, Millie and Moose looked at each other for a long time without speaking. Then Moose said, "You really think he'd offer forty thousand?"

"It's a lot of money," Millie said.

"Christ, what I could do with forty thousand."

"Why don't you see if it'll buy you another post office?"

One morning nearly two weeks after Mrs. Keller had moved away, Sorenson drove through the town in the Chevrolet, the red flags on the front fenders alternately limp and stiff in the wind. In less than ten minutes Simmer was heading up the main road after him at what seemed like a hundred and fifty miles an hour. He found Sorenson sitting in the station wagon in front of Mrs. Keller's house.

"Can you beat this weather?" Sorenson said as Simmer walked up beside the car.

"I give you credit," Simmer told him. "I didn't think you were that smart."

"The house?" he said. "That's routine."

"That and being gone for two weeks."

"There are right-of-way problems with a group of residences just outside Portsmouth," Sorenson answered.

"What did you do to them?"

"None of your business," he said. He got out of the car and leaned back against the door. Simmer took a position alongside of Sorenson, and together they stared at Mrs. Keller's house. "A pretty place," Sorenson said. "There's strength to that house." He regarded it in a curious way, half in admiration of its architecture and half in consideration of where the wrecking ball would strike it first.

"What'd you pay for it?" Simmer asked.

"Fair market value would be a point or two under

eighteen." Simmer nodded. "Well, the old lady didn't get that. It's not how I work. You see," he said and turned slightly toward Simmer, "I start the offers high, and as they are rejected and as time goes by I lower them."

"In other words, you punish people."

"If I worked any other way I'd still be negotiating my first acquisition," Sorenson said.

"How long you got for this one?"

"Years, if need be." There was a short pause before Sorenson went on. "Before this is all over, I imagine we'll know one another pretty well."

"Don't count on it."

They continued to stand against the car, their arms folded tight across their chests, looking at Mrs. Keller's house. From a distance, except for the way they were dressed, they looked like twins.

Simmer was the first to see the flatbed truck with the bulldozer on it turn the corner off Route 10 and grind its way toward them. He watched as Sorenson waved the truck to the other side of the road, where it stopped with the wheels on its left side fully on the lawn. Instantly they sank several inches deep in the fresh short grass. Sorenson went directly to the driver and gave him instructions to unload the bulldozer. Then he came back and stood next to Simmer without either speaking or looking at him.

The driver unhooked the safety chains and vaulted into the seat of the bulldozer. He backed it down off the small ramp at the rear of the truck, and with a quick, chugging swivel he turned it toward the house and drove it across the lawn. For an instant Simmer thought he was going straight into the living room, but just when he reached the lilac bushes near the front door he stopped the machine, pivoted it sharply on the fine grass, and then looked back to Sorenson for directions. Sorenson dropped his hand in a solid flat motion, and simultane-

66

ously the driver hit the hydraulic lever that dropped the blade quickly and solidly into the lawn. Then he shut off the engine, went back to the truck, and drove it off.

"What are you going to do with that?" Simmer asked slowly.

"Nice, don't you think?"

"I do not."

"You'll get used to it," Sorenson said. "It's to let people know I'm here to stay."

Simmer looked away from him to where the bulldozer tracks had torn up the spring lawn. The sharp cleats in the tracks had neatly parceled out the turf in small rectangular sections, and each of the little fragments lay across the lawn humped and paralyzed, as though finally ready for transplant.

The men stood together for another few minutes; then, without speaking, Simmer moved off to his truck. As he went, Sorenson called to him, "I'm prepared to make you an offer for your business and your land."

Simmer half-turned and said over his shoulder, "Not interested."

There was a strange quality to the sound of what Simmer said. It was as though nothing in the world could have been any truer. And when Sorenson called back, "You will be," his voice was hollow and empty, as if he were quoting livestock prices or giving out some meaningless weights and measures.

As Simmer drove slowly past him and down the street toward the post office, Sorenson called, "Next offer's lower, you know." But Simmer did not hear him, and Sorenson knew that even if he had, it would have made no difference.

Sorenson stood for a moment like an empty-handed child whose candy has just been snatched away. Then suddenly, viciously angry, he went to the back of the station wagon where under a canvas tarpaulin lay the jackhammer, several brand-new pickaxes, and a gleaming chain saw. With ease he snatched the saw out of the back, then held it close to him while he checked the oil and gas chambers. Then he went directly to the old spruce that stood to one side of Mrs. Keller's house. He knelt and put one foot through the metal handle of the chain saw. One pull on the starter rope, and the machine came to life. As it idled it sounded like the rapid heart-beat of a wild metallic animal, and when Sorenson pressed the trigger the chain began to whirl with an enormous din, its roar rolling out and over the whole town and for what seemed many miles beyond. The deep charging sound gave way to a high-pitched whine as the saw slid into the trunk of the tree. Chips of fresh oily wood flew up at Sorenson and bounced from his arms and chest. Then the clean sawdust ran from the tree like a stream of milk, making a small neat pile on the ground. Sorenson went through the trunk without stopping, without letting up even for an instant, and when the tree fell it did so almost silently and lay for a moment in disorganized quiverings in front of the house. Quickly Sorenson attacked it. He stripped its branches literally by walking its length several times, and then with great precision he began to lop the trunk into two-foot lengths.

While Sorenson was venting his anger on the old spruce tree, The Reverend Mr. Barker drove by on his way home from the post office. When he saw Sorenson, Barker slowed his car to a crawl and almost smiled at him. He sensed a deep personal irony in Sorenson's presence, both at town meeting and now on another day that was meaningful to him. The night of town meeting the minister in Newfield had suffered a major stroke, and although Barker did not find out about it until the following afternoon, he had known instantly that his call to Newfield was then only a matter of time. Just minutes before he drove past Sorenson as he mutilated the tree in front of Mrs. Keller's house, he had gotten the call. It had come, though, in a form he had not immediately liked. The letter he received had assigned him the post of "Acting Curate" in Newfield, and it had gone on to say that, ". . . the duties and responsibilities of your own church will necessarily still be in effect, at least until such time as the situation in Newfield receives proper resolution and an appropriate replacement is found for you."

Barker watched Sorenson with a mixture of awe and distant affection, almost as if in some strange way he owed him his call to Newfield, and in a spontaneous gesture he raised his hand from the steering wheel, and before he realized what he had done he waved to Sorenson. As he drove on, the letter from his superior lying open on the seat beside him like some special passenger, he felt an open contempt for the town and those he had been forced to serve for nineteen years. All of his hopes were suddenly as alive as the fresh spring morning, and with enormous pleasure he thought back to the long graveside sermon he had given for Mr. Keller. It had been a moment of solid fulfillment, and he knew that the sermon he had delivered was certainly one of his very best, certainly worthy of the Newfield church. It seemed to him that he had been able to comfort the whole town with his suddenly distilled concept of the meaning of life itself. He had called life a "glorious synthesis," a "spectacular, divine harmony," and he had even comforted the townspeople about Sorenson's news by saying, "The future holds for us all a reward the likes of which we are powerless to determine, powerless to comprehend."

As he drove on he composed the letter he would write to his superior that evening. He really wished he could handwrite it, to make it as beautiful an object to look at as it would be to read. In it he would state his gratitude for his new position, declare with all the verbal ability he could manage his understanding of his new double duties, and then he would end with a true flourish of humility. It would be like one of his better sermons, the kind he reserved for summer Sundays in Newfield.

When he got back to his house, Ellen Thomas was waiting for him on the steps. As he stopped the car she turned to face him. "Wonderful news," he said, and he held up the letter inside the car. He got out quickly and went toward her.

"I've got to talk to you," she said.

"I've got the letter," he said. He reached out as if to hold her by the shoulders, but then he stopped.

"Something's wrong with Culver," she said. Her eyes looked dead, as if they had over the years become old brown bullet holes.

"Come in, come in," Barker said. As he opened the door for her he put the letter in his inside pocket.

They sat in the living room still in their coats, and every now and again Barker moved his hand over the letter. It was the kind of room that, even with the tall spacious windows on three sides, seemed to get no light at all. The one dominant color in it was a dark gray that seemed to have come upon the room slowly over the years Barker had lived there. There were a couple of old paintings on the walls, a sickened dirty fireplace, and thick cobwebs in every corner of the ceiling.

"I can't talk to him anymore," Ellen said. "He's become someone I've never known." Barker nodded and smiled warmly at her. "You know what he does?" Barker raised his eyebrows for her to go on. "He's been walking all over the house all night long," she said. "With one of those awful shotguns of his."

"Is it loaded?"

"Of course it's loaded."

"Surely you've reasoned with him," Barker said. He was suddenly more annoyed than concerned.

"Once," she answered, "and he pointed the thing right at me and ordered me back to bed." She stopped

70

then for a moment as though to assess how she felt after telling about it. Then she said in what seemed to be a final conclusion, "I think he might shoot me."

Barker's smile was huge on his face. "Mr. Sorenson has upset us all," he told Ellen.

"I just want to pack up everything," she said and she looked toward the window, "every last stick in the house, and go home to Newfield."

"And Culver says no?"

"He's insane about it."

"You could go," Barker said.

Ellen was silent for a few moments, and then she said, "I might have to."

Ever since Sorenson had bought out Mrs. Keller, Culver had gone to bed each night relaxed and sleepy. But no sooner had his head touched the pillow than his mind turned into a private slide show of town meeting and all the events since. As if in some accompaniment to the pictures his mind threw against the blackness of the bedroom, his heart would imperceptibly pick up its pace and begin to run all by itself into a pounding that finally frightened Culver so much that, to distract himself from it, he would get up. The first few nights, he sat in the living room and watched the last bits and fragments of the fire turn to white ash. On nights when there was no fire Culver went to his chair by the window and looked out over the town. There was an utter peace and shadowy tranquillity to the town late at night, and Culver saw the massive black outlines of the houses as things as permanent as life itself. As hard as he tried, he found it impossible to see the houses suddenly gone and in their place the high sleek parallels of the interstate vaulting across the valley.

After the first week, Culver took to getting his shotgun down from the gun rack next to the front door and holding it across his lap as he sat by the window, and occasionally he imagined he saw the outlines of figures coming down the street like soldiers, and more than once he quickly moved to the back of the house to see if they had gone around there. But the moonlight was never right back there; the trees were heavy and dense, and from the windows in the back he was never able to see anything at all.

Finally, one night long past midnight Culver was holding the gun tightly across his knees, and as though in a moment of fantastic conclusion he snapped the weapon to his shoulder and aimed it out the window. "I'll kill you, you son of a bitch," he said out loud, and he squeezed both triggers together. They made a loud, stupid sound in the room, like two metal teeth hitting each other at random, and Culver held the gun to his shoulder for a few moments more. Then he slowly brought it down, the butt end sliding into his belly, his hands tight around the barrels, and he leaned his head gently on his hands. He was horrified for a moment that in his silent lonely rage he could actually have killed, and he sat as though in a prayer of repentance. But under his hands he smelled the metallic oily residue of thousands of gunshots, and in a strange way that had never happened before, the smell made his mouth water.

Ellen Thomas

If you lived in Newfield, the chances were that at one time or another your ancestors had lived in Oldenfield. The relationship between the two towns was one of quiet hostility, as though Newfield were the castle, Oldenfield the place where the serfs lived. Newfield was an extremely prosperous town, and over the years it had sucked dry the better and more ambitious young people in Oldenfield. And when an Oldenfield resident married, it was almost always to someone in Newfield, and, in what seemed an integral part of the ceremony, that person moved to Newfield. That alone made Ellen Niles's marriage to Culver Thomas unusual. It was assumed, what with Ellen's father being as prominent as he was in Newfield, that Culver would move there to become involved in his construction business. But Culver had been emphatic—some said downright pigheaded—about Ellen's coming to live in Oldenfield, and when Ellen's father had asked her why in the world she wanted to go down there and live with those people, she had dutifully answered because it's where Culver is. It was also because she was thoroughly desperate to marry. She was twenty-eight and, as she had assessed herself one time, getting dumpier every day. But she was not so much ugly as in possession of a quality beyond ugliness. She was bland and insignificant, with no feature of her face or body either pleasing or repulsive. She looked as if she had been made up from the mediocre parts of other people. Her eyes sat in her head with what seemed a clear paste over them; her nose was straight but quite small, her mouth a thin expressionless slit across her face. Her body had the character of the aging choir girl that she was, its top part seemingly stuck forcibly into the lower. Her plain dresses always fell nearly to mid-calf, and from there her legs ran straight into her shoes in a way that suggested she had never grown ankles.

But Ellen Thomas could sing. From the time she was nine years old she had sung in the Newfield Baptist church and at every school function where she could be worked in. Her voice was a unique one, not so much pure as it was true. When she sang, Ellen produced the effect that she fully understood all the feelings and emotions behind every word in every song. One had the sensation that somehow she had gathered together worlds of experience and compressed them all into each song. But Ellen was not conscious of her abilities, of the overall impact she had on the church and school audiences, and often, as she sang in a way that moved an entire congregation, she was thinking of a book on sewing she wanted, a geography assignment, or the wet shiny arms and legs of the basketball players she had watched the afternoon before.

She stopped singing when she married Culver. In fact, because of him she stopped going to church at all, and it wasn't until her son had been killed that she began to sing again, began to go back to the church as though looking for something lost for so long that there was some question that it had ever existed at all. But after her seven years' absence, something had happened to her voice. It was as if it and something fragile inside her had changed ever so slightly, moved just that little bit off perfect center. The quality of her voice was still thrilling to hear, but when she thought hard about the hymns she sang, one had the feeling that she was pushing the song out of her in an effort to convince herself that the words were true.

Sorenson was at the post office a few minutes after seven, and Moose Krause was terrified when he saw him walk in. "I want a box rental," Sorenson said.

"Two dollars a year," Moose answered; "fifty cents the quarter." He looked up to a sheet that was pinned inside the window where he stood. "Only I've got nothing now."

Sorenson looked at him and smiled. Then he turned and looked at the far wall where a hundred mailboxes sat dark and empty. "No," Moose said, "they've been discontinued. They're all out of service."

"I assumed that Mrs. Keller's was available."

"It don't automatically come with the house," Moose replied. He suddenly felt in supreme control of Sorenson.

"But it is free."

"She's paid up through August. It's hers till then."

Without a word Sorenson turned from the little window and began to move about the small lobby. He went to the front window and ran his hand along the casement seams, pushed lightly on the windowpanes to test the molding, and then walked over the floor in small steps looking for weak places. He paused by the door to examine the weatherstripping, checked the hinges, and then methodically began to tap the old paneling that covered the side walls. His eyes went over the light fixtures, noting how they were set in the walls, and when his gaze came to rest on the giant head of the Canadian moose he broke out laughing. "Where the hell did you ever get that?"

"I shot it," Moose said, "right between its goddamn eyes."

Sorenson walked over to it and carefully examined it. He raised one hand and let it run over the dusty, thinned-out fur. "Thirty-ought-six at about fifty yards," he said.

"More like seventy-five," Moose said. "You can get your mail at the window."

"Top dollar," Sorenson suddenly exploded. "First offer is top dollar."

"I don't give a damn what your first offer is." He opened the drawer at his waist and began sorting stamps into silly meaningless piles.

"There's five rooms upstairs," Sorenson declared. "Forced hot water, half acre in back; assessment's fourteen thousand." His eyes blinked hard and fast as he registered each calculation. "Now tell me what you'd take for everything."

"She's not for sale," Moose said.

"Everything is for sale," Sorenson said. "Houses, land, people, everything."

"You speak for yourself."

"I'll tell you right now that you're going to lose a lot of money." He paused and looked past Moose to survey the back part of the post office. "And a lot of other people in this town are going to lose a lot of money."

"You can get your mail at the window," Moose repeated. He looked out the large front window as Millie's jeep pulled in.

"My offer's fifty-two thousand dollars," Sorenson suddenly blurted, "but you've got to let me know by seven this evening." He turned and went quickly to the door. When he saw Millie, he pulled open the door and held it back for her. "Good morning," he said. "I shall be coming to see you in due time."

"Come anywhere near my store and I'll bust open your head," she said, going past him like an angry bull.

"Seven tonight," Sorenson called to Moose, and then he was out the door.

"And just what the hell did he want?" Millie asked.

"He made me an offer," Moose answered. In his voice there was utter shock and bewilderment. It was as if only then had he really heard Sorenson's figure. "Simmer's right," Moose said as though to himself. "He's got real money."

"I'd bet he wouldn't give over twenty-five," Millie said.

"That's because you don't know nothing about real estate," Moose told her. "All you've ever known was that store. If you had any sense you'd of developed it, added onto it, made some improvements like I done here."

"He offer you Fort Knox?"

"He offered me, if it's any of your business, fifty-two thousand dollars."

It was as if Moose had thrown a rock at Millie and hit her squarely in the face. She was visibly staggered by the figure. In an effort to comfort her, Moose leaned out of his window as if he were going to kiss her. "Your place has got to be worth a bundle," he said.

Millie looked at him for a long moment, her eyes

sweeping his face very rapidly. Finally she said, "I need three air mails and three regulars." While Moose fumbled in the stamp drawer Millie said directly, "Are you going to take it?"

"Who knows?"

"You goddamn liar," she said.

"You just think I got too much," he said. He slid the stamps to her, and without looking at him she put down the precise change and left the post office.

Several other people came in during the next hour, two to collect their mail, and one, Calvin Runners, to mail a package to his sister in Boston. Moose said nothing about Sorenson to any of them, but then after another hour or so no one came to the post office. It did not immediately register with Moose that people had not come in the late morning as they usually did, but he was genuinely puzzled when he closed for lunch and only seven people, including Sorenson, had come in all morning.

After lunch, and shortly after he had sorted the afternoon mail, Moose suddenly became afraid. He left the back of the post office and went quickly to the front door, opening it wide and fixing it so that it would stay open. It was very much like an invitation he was giving to all the world to come and have a visit with him, and even though the sky was heaped with gray clouds and the wind rustled with a moist cold bite, Moose kept the door open for over an hour. When he finally had to close it, he did so with an attitude that was clearly open defeat. He realized that Millie had spread the word on him, and there was a sick feeling all through him when he finally closed the post office at five o'clock. He felt guilty and contrite all at once, and where the figure of fifty-two thousand dollars had during the morning jumped and dazzled in his mind, it was now like a great acid weight churning in his belly.

When he went upstairs to his apartment, he looked around in a way he had not done since his wife had died.

Then in a flash that scared him he wondered how Sorenson had known there were five rooms above the post office. He went to the little writing desk that had been his wife's and took out a bottle of whiskey. He poured himself two quick shots and then took a pencil and began to write figures on the back of an envelope. He put down his savings, his income from his government pension, his life insurance, Social Security, what he estimated he could get for his furniture, tools, even his car. Then he put down Sorenson's figure and added it up. "My God," he said to the empty room. "I could be rich." He was looking at a figure of just under ninety thousand dollars.

As he sat there alone in the dim light of the room, he did not at first hear the rain begin a light steady beating on the low roof above his head. But after a few moments the sound grew more intense, more insistent, and suddenly a great mellow wave swept through him, and for the first time in many, many years he consciously missed his wife. He listened to the sound of the rain on the shingles; then, mixed with that sound, there came the heavier sound of the water beginning to run off the sides of the roof and hit the pieces of worn flagstone that ringed the building.

Moose sat there for a long time, alternately listening hard to the different rain sounds and letting himself float helplessly back to some of the good days he had had with his wife and family. Then it seemed to him that his whole life had been spent fighting things that had never had a name, things that had gushed through him and poured out on other people, things without meaning or purpose. It was as though he saw his past made up of ten thousand tiny fires, and that in each of them he had wasted a small part of himself. He looked down again at the paper with the figures on it and then crumpled it in his hand and tossed it aside. He rose from his chair and went to the front part of the living room. He stood in front of the middle window and looked out into the early evening settling in with the rain. From the second story of the post office much of the town was visible, and Moose stood there a long time looking at it with an affection he had not known he still had. Finally, he turned away and took his coat from the back of an old overstuffed chair that had been his wife's favorite and started for the door. The envelope lay in a wad on the floor in front of him, and as he kicked it out of the way he muttered, "I'm crazy."

When Moose had suspected that afternoon that Millie had put the word out on him, he was absolutely right. What he did not know, though, was how swift and with what delight she had done it. Within an hour of leaving the post office, she had called everyone she could think of in the town. As she related it, it was no rumor. She told people that Moose had sold out to the state lock, stock and barrel, and that he had told her to do the same thing.

What Millie did not reveal was the size of Sorenson's offer to Moose. Had she done so, the reactions of the people she called would have been a good deal more mixed. When asked how much Moose had gotten from the state, Millie said she didn't know but that so far as she was concerned Moose had probably sold out for two shiny dimes. When she called Culver, Ellen answered the phone and said that Culver had gone to Newfield. Millie told her, "You tell him that Moose went and sold out to Sorenson." There was a long pause while Millie waited for Ellen's reaction. Finally, Millie said, "Well, what do you think of that?"

"To be frank," Ellen answered, "he's the only person in this whole town with any sense in his head."

"You just tell Culver," Millie said.

Next Millie called Simmer, who said it's what you could have expected of Moose right from the start. Hal

Bitterley called Moose a no-good bastard, and Calvin Runners said, "My old lady'll kill him when she gets wind of it."

But the reactions Millie got over the telephone did nothing to still her rage. Instead of feeling her anger spread out and diminish in a shared kind of way, it was as though each reaction multiplied her feelings and focused them even more intensely on Moose. When she put down the receiver after her last call, she felt about Moose the same way she felt about Sorenson.

As she stood next to the phone behind the counter, she had been holding a can of soup in her right hand. All through the calls she had squeezed it as hard as she could, and now she saw that the paper label had come off and lay curled at her feet.

When Jerky came out of the back with sleep in soft lumps all over his face, and his fatigues rumpled and creased from the bed, Millie did not immediately see him. When she did, she looked at him in disgust. She held the can of soup in her hand like a baseball she was readying to throw at him. Finally, she slammed it down on the counter and said, "Do you have any idea in the world what time it is?"

Jerky ignored her, going to the bread display, where he poked about in the doughnuts and pastries. When he had selected what he wanted, he simply put a finger through the thin plastic covering of the top and drew it back. He took out a doughnut and began to eat it.

"You want something," Millie said, "you pay for it."

"Dry up."

"I'm going to start keeping a bill on you." She leaned forward on the counter, and for just an instant her locked arms looked like short, misplaced legs. "I've got things for you to do, you know."

"I'm going into the woods," he said, taking another doughnut and putting almost half of it into his mouth.

"Sorenson bought out Moose this morning," Millie suddenly said.

"Big deal." Jerky answered as if he had for a long time expected the news. He turned fully toward his mother. "If a man offers you money for something worthless," he said, "you'd better take it."

"Why are you going into the woods?"

"To kill warm and furry things," he answered. "Robins, squirrels, things like that." Going to the back of the store, he slid back the glass doors of the beverage case, took out a quart of chocolate milk and opened it. Millie watched in silence as he drank most of it without stopping for breath. When he took the container from his mouth he said to her, "Black flies. For God's sake, I've got to know when the black flies are coming out."

"It's damn well time you did some work and earned your keep around here," she told him.

"Not on your life," he said. "I'm owed."

Black flies are only a little larger than gnats, and their life span, give or take a wet or dry month, is not much longer than six weeks. If it were much longer, say seasonal, almost all of northern New England would be unfit for humans. The reason is simple: black flies need a bite from a warm-blooded animal in order to reproduce and lay their eggs in the run-off streams for the following year. The one thing that attracts them, something on the order of an appetizer, is sweat, and they can sense it from miles away. Like a million tiny sharks they can zero in on a human being and almost literally drive him mad. In their enormous sexual thirst for blood they will fly into the mouth, nose, ears, and eyes, and even from some distance away they are visible as they hover and swirl about a person's head. The bite of the black fly is sometimes quite painful, but it is nothing in comparison to what will follow in a few hours, and within the day a core will form so hard that it is like suddenly having a pebble growing under the skin.

But black flies do not for some reason affect everyone the same way; they discriminate. In droves they seek out those people they can literally make ill with one bite. Others, to whom a black fly bite is nothing more than a slight irritation, go through the whole six weeks' season without so much as mentioning them. Jerky Barnhope was among the former group, and every other day for the last two weeks he had carefully measured the temperature of the run-off streams in the woods behind the store. At a little over thirty-eight degrees the black flies hatch, and the last temperature of the water had been almost thirty-seven.

As Jerky went out the front door, he saw Sorenson walking a little way ahead of him. As if he felt Jerky's eyes on his back, Sorenson turned around and looked at him. Jerky felt a strange, eerie rising in his belly, a flood of uncontrollable anger that seemed for an instant to sear and choke him all at once. Sorenson nodded to him and raised his hand slightly, then turned and strolled on up the road in a way that said he didn't care whether Jerky lived or died. Jerky watched him for a few moments; then he turned and snatched the thermometer from its metal clamp and studied it. The air temperature was forty-two, although for some indefinable reason the morning felt much warmer. He put the instrument into his fatigues pocket and started around toward the back of the store. With unusual grace he lightly hopscotched several large rocks in the stream, and then he was gone into the woods just on the other side.

Jerky moved quickly and easily through the woods, and even in places where the underbrush had grown thick and dense he seemed to pass through it without disturbing it. He concentrated on his direction and speed, and when he got to the first little run-off stream, he saw that there was still a good swift current in it. He put the thermometer in the water and watched it, warm and near sixty degrees from his body heat, begin to drop fast. It began to slow up at forty-four and crept ever slower to forty-one. When it seemed to stop there, Jerky shoved it deeper into the water, as if through his own will power he would drive the temperature down. Simultaneously with the realization that the water temperature was at least two full degrees above that needed for hatching, Jerky heard the first black fly near his right ear. Seemingly crazed, the fly dove into his ear as far as it could go, its light persistent buzzing exploding in Jerky's head. Then several flew directly in front of his eyes, some hovering in front of his nostrils, and when he opened his mouth slightly in surprise, immediately five or six settled on his tongue and the insides of his lips. Then, suddenly, they were all about his head like a great gauze hood. Frantically he waved his hands and beat the air around him, but all his efforts and strength seemed only to multiply the numbers that swarmed around him. With a small half groan that came from somewhere far deeper than his throat, Jerky was up and running for all he was worth.

When he got back to the edge of the stream that ran just behind the store, he stopped and stood looking back at the woods as if the flies had forcibly ejected him. His face looked as if someone had shotgunned it with red ink. There were two kinds of blood on it. Where the tree branches had snapped along his face, there were small whiplike scratches, and interwoven with the scratches were little shattered bubbles of blood that stuck to his skin. The flies having stopped for the moment in the safety of the woods, Jerky stood with his chest heaving from his long run. But then, as his breath came back, the buzzing around his ears heightened, and all at once he drew several flies all the way into his lungs. He retched and spat several times and then fell to his knees by the edge of the stream. He had drunk from it for a few seconds before he realized that every handful of water he brought to his mouth contained black flies. Getting to his feet, he carefully stepped across the rocks and onto the other side. He walked the thirty or so yards to the house very slowly, as though to tell the flies that he had given up the fight against them, and when he had almost reached the back porch they abandoned him.

On the way to Millie's store that evening Moose stopped his car in front of Sorenson's house. There was a small dim light on in the back of the house, but when Moose shut off the engine, lights came on all over the front almost instantly. Then the porch light snapped on and Sorenson's head appeared between the curtains in the living room. Moose got out of the car and walked straight to the front door. He banged on it twice and immediately heard Sorenson's voice from the other side. "Who's there?"

"Krause."

"And you want?"

"I've made up my mind about the house," Moose said. There was a pause while Sorenson opened first the chain lock, then a bolt, and finally another lock. Moose laughed as the door slid open. "What you got all them locks for?"

"My safety is my concern," Sorenson said. Only the top of his head and his two hard eyes showed around the crack in the door.

"Look, I'm not selling," Moose suddenly blurted, and upon hearing his own words he felt great relief. Quickly he added, "Now or ever."

Moose expected an immediate and direct response, even a threat, but Sorenson only stood in the pale light looking past Moose and on across the street. There was a long time in which he seemed to be considering the future. Finally he said in a clipped, almost satisfied tone, "Thank you very much."

"What are you going to do?" Moose asked in a surprised, somewhat childish way.

"Thank you very much," Sorenson said again. This time he closed the door, and the locks fell into place as though manipulated by more than two hands. Before Moose could turn and start down the steps, the porch light was out, and so were the others in the front part of the house. As he got back into his car he had the strange sensation that he had never even talked to Sorenson.

Moose was not surprised a few minutes later to see both Simmer's and Culver's pickup trucks parked outside Millie's store. What did surprise him was Barker's car parked between them. In a sudden moment of elation Moose hit the horn of his car in an attempt to announce to those in the store that he had arrived and to tell them that he had turned down Sorenson's offer. As he went up the steps he saw Millie pull down the window shade that covered the front door. He stood for a moment facing the red CLOSED sign painted on it. Then he knocked hard and waited. When no one came he knocked again.

Millie's voice came loud and strong: "You're not welcome in this store, Moose Krause."

"You open up," Moose shouted back.

"Go count your money."

Moose began to kick at the door with such force that it threatened to give way. "You got no right to say that," he hollered. He kicked harder.

"All right, all right," Simmer yelled. He opened the door a crack and said to Moose, "Do you want to show us your check?"

"I'll show you the end of my boot," Moose said as he charged past him and toward the counter where Millie and Culver stood.

"I got a right to close my store when I want," Millie said.

"You do like hell!" Moose shouted as if he were still on the other side of the door. "Now what've you gone

85

and told everybody?" He was leaning on the counter, his face not more than two feet from Millie's.

"The truth, you cheap bastard," she said.

"If you were a man I'd punch your fat face," he said. Then quickly and easily he spun around next to the counter and faced Culver and Simmer. His eyes stayed on them for a few seconds, and then he glanced at Barker standing a little behind the stove. As if he were an experienced orator he said, "I told the son of a bitch no." Without waiting for a response he shoved off from the counter and swaggered back to the beverage case, sliding the door back hard and letting it bang. Then he reached inside, took out a quart bottle of beer, twisted off the cap and took a long drink. With the bottle to his mouth he heard Simmer say, "Sorenson's taking Grasston."

"But it's south," Millie said.

"Got to be at least twelve, fifteen miles from the right-of-way," Culver put in.

"He's taking it for the gravel it sits on," Simmer told them. "Buying the whole town is cheaper than trucking in from downstate."

"But where does he get the right?" Millie said, suddenly near panic. "Where does he get the *legal* right?"

"Eminent domain," Simmer said very quietly. "With reason enough Sorenson could take Concord or Manchester."

The rain that had begun late in the afternoon now rose in force against the sturdy little building, and the wind howled and moaned as if it were trying to get into the store. For a few moments they all seemed to be listening to it, and then finally, as if making a pronouncement, Barker said, "They say we're in for a blow."

"It's likely," Simmer said without interest.

No one took any notice of Jerky as he came out of the back of the store and went to the beverage case. He took out a six-pack of beer and turned toward the others. For

86

a moment he studied them, their faces seemingly spread with ashes, their bodies hunched and sunken as though weighted down. "What's the matter?" he said. "Somebody die?"

"In a way," Barker answered.

"Profound, Mr. Reverino," Jerky said. "And with what other words will you comfort us this evening?"

"Shut up," Millie threw at him.

"Look at yourself," Barker snapped. "You're nothing but a silly little boy who can't stop playing soldier." He paused as his eyes swept Jerky. "I'm just glad there aren't any children in this town. What a terrible example you are."

"Did you ever kill anybody?" Jerky asked softly.

"Yes," Culver interrupted. "A soldier from Aachen. He was about your age."

"How?" Jerky said. His eyes darted about the room.

"I marched him over a little hill, chatting all the way," Culver said, "and then I blew his head off."

"Dear God," Barker whispered.

"I got to be going," Jerky said. He pulled the six-pack to him and very quickly was gone into the shadows in the back of the store.

For several hours Jerky drank the beer and smoked his joints, but his mind stayed remarkably clear. When he had almost finished his six-pack, he got off his bed and carefully smoothed out his fatigues. He tucked his shirt into his trousers and pulled it down tight, as if readying himself for immediate inspection. Next he did his boots, offering them more of a drool than a spit shine, and when he was satisfied, he went to the basement and brought up his foul-weather gear. He arranged it on his bed and then checked it against some mental list. He counted things, double-checked, and finally said out loud, "Yes, *sir.*"

Jerky was a funny sight in his poncho and fatigue hat

as he left the small back porch. Within two steps he was as wet from the rain as if he had been outside for hours, and the poncho gleamed in the soft yellow light that oozed from the small store windows. He walked quickly up the main street toward Sorenson's house, his step ever quicker and more determined the closer he got. In his own mind, Jerky was on patrol. When he saw Sorenson's house clearly, he stopped and took cover next to a large oak. Occasionally, a strong gust of wind brought the rain up and across his face in a slow and thorough caress. The house blurred and wavered in Jerky's vision, and several times he had to wipe his face hard and, like a child, dig the water from his eyes with his small fists.

He stood there for a long time, choosing the trees and utility poles he would use for cover as he made his way toward the house. Then, in a glistening little flash, he was off and running on his route. He paused at each of the spots he had picked, and then in a second or two he was on to the next one. He finally threw himself to the ground just behind the bulldozer that sat on Sorenson's front lawn. His knees dug so far into the soft turf that he lost his balance and tipped forward. His arms and face splashed into the wet soil, and a fine spray flew up around his head. He cursed and then quickly moved forward to the edge of the bulldozer. He crouched there for a few moments, his hand on the top edge of the blade, and looked around. He checked the house, and when he found all still quiet he slowly pivoted in his crouched position and looked up and down the street. When he looked back toward the house, the reflection of a distant street light caught itself like a jewel in the blade of the bulldozer, and he saw that the whole metal surface was highly polished. He was even able to see a faint reflection of himself in it.

He stood up a little and looked over the blade and past the huge metal cleats in the tracks. His eyes swept the large yard swiftly, and almost instantly he knew that the only genuine cover in the whole place was the bulldozer itself. As if he were crawling into a hole, Jerky squatted, dropped to all fours, and eased himself under the machine. He dragged himself across the soft wet ground on his elbows until he could get a clear view of the house. He lay there for a moment, and then his legs snapped out to the sides and his hands folded out in front of him as though to hold a rifle. He held the prone position for several moments, and patiently he sighted along the imaginary barrel. His head moved slightly as his arms swung in position from one window to the next, eyes searching for Sorenson's figure.

Then suddenly Jerky realized that he was lying in an ever-deepening pool of water that spread past his spot under the bulldozer and widened out into a large oval area that covered nearly half the yard. Cursing, he began to ease himself back down through the water and out from under the front end of the bulldozer. He stood up and for a moment seemed to be trying to stare Sorenson's house out of existence. Then he turned and began to walk away from the house without trying to conceal himself, almost hoping in fact that Sorenson was at a window watching his every move.

Just when it seemed as if the rain could not possibly come down harder, it somehow renewed itself, became heavier and more insistent. When the storm was only half over, the people in the town knew that it was the kind they would talk about for years to come. Late that night, when all of the lights of the town were out except Sorenson's, the rain seemed to multiply in intensity, and a swirling wind began to blow. It was a strange wind, one that never stopped, that ignored the rules and blew straight and hard without a gust. It drove the rain first against the houses and then seemingly into the very sidings themselves. The wood seemed to swell and groan silently as though some fierce aging process were racing ahead completely out of control. The trees leaned sideways: the heavier ones stiff and full of tension; the slighter, younger ones almost trying to reach the ground to escape the wind. It was as if a great power were at work, and through the night little bedroom lights dotted on throughout the town as people woke from the wind hurling the rain in great punches against the houses.

The morning broke very late and with a deep grayness. The wind seemed to have slipped away beyond the mountain, but the rain still came in thick and heavy sheets. The streets were a shambles of small natural ruins. All over, there were thick green leaves lying in soggy piles by the sides of the roads, and little trees and branches that had been new growth that spring lay scattered across the lawns. The whole town would have had the look of late autumn had it not been for the dark green color of the fallen leaves and the tenderness of the sheared twigs and branches.

There was not much activity in the town that morning. People stayed in their houses for the most part, and those who did go out bundled heavily against the rain. In the post office people stayed much longer than usual, and they talked only of the damage the storm had so far done to their houses. When Millie came in she was quick to announce that the stream behind her store was a raging torrent, and that if the rain did not let up by afternoon, the water in the pond would be dangerously high. "There's nothing under the sun that'll keep that pond in its banks," Millie said to Moose.

"Hal Bitterley said Prior Lake's churned up like he never seen it," Moose said. There was a vacant, flat tone to his voice, but when everyone but Millie was gone from the post office he changed his tone. "I think Sorenson's gone crazy. He drove up here this morning and stopped his car right out in front. He never even got out of it."

Millie was holding up the envelopes to the light and reading the amounts of the bills. "He just sat there for half an hour and made notes on a clipboard."

"Maybe he's figuring another offer," Millie said.

"Not after last night," Moose answered with great pride. "He knew I meant what I said."

"Look at this damn thing," Millie suddenly blurted. She brought the long envelope down from her eyes and ripped it open. "That goddamn dairy is in for it this time." She flipped the statement flat in her hand. "I thought that's what the thing said. Do you know what I make on a quart of milk?" Moose shrugged. "Next to goddamn nothing." In a gesture that made Moose step back a little Millie crushed the bill in her hand and flung it as hard as she could toward the waist-high trash basket in the far corner. "I'll tell you one thing," she snapped at Moose, "and that's if Sorenson were here now I'd let him have the whole thing." She moved her hands like an umpire giving a safe sign. "The whole thing," she said again.

The rain did not let up all during the day, and shortly before dark the water in the pond behind Millie's store slid out of its banks and quickly spread across her lawn and around the house. After half an hour it was past her house and into the street, where it formed first a small, fast-moving stream and then a larger one that seemed to feed on its own momentum. It wound down through the main street of the town, zigzagging with the grade of the road toward Simmer's Garage. It broke there into two sections: one was a light, slow trickle that finally puddled itself beyond the gas station; the other, growing angrier by the minute, dove across Route 10 and burrowed its way into Prior Lake. Within an hour both streams were running a dark brown from the soil they carried away from the town.

When Jerky left the store that evening with his rifle under his poncho, the water in the yard was well past his ankles. But he went through it without taking any notice. His feet made little splashes of light in the water, but he kept on as if under orders. In the middle of the street he turned sharply left and began to double-time up the road toward Sorenson's house. He followed the same route he had traced out the night before, and only once did he have to flatten himself behind a tree to avoid the clean white lights of a passing car. He stopped just on the other side of the street from Sorenson's house and studied the lighting pattern in the windows. It was the same as the night before, and Jerky waited for a few minutes to catch Sorenson's silhouette behind the living room window. He saw that Sorenson was moving in a quick, determined pattern throughout the whole downstairs, and after another moment Jerky took the rifle from under his poncho and checked the magazine. He carefully looked up and down the street, and then in an instant he ran across the road and flung himself down beside the blade of the bulldozer.

He crawled forward on his elbows and knees, the rifle cradled in the crooks of his arms. He was very low under the bulldozer, and the top of his head scraped along its massive underbelly. When he looked up over the rifle he saw Sorenson's house framed by the ends of the two giant tracks that sat deep and heavy in the very soft wet soil. He froze where he was as Sorenson's dark profile slid by one of the dining room windows and then stopped, framed perfectly by one of the kitchen windows. Jerky snapped the rifle into place with as much ease and assurance as if he had been practicing daily since he left the army. He sighted the rifle along the window where Sorenson stood and squeezed off an imaginary round. "Pow," he said out loud. Then quickly, "Pow, pow." His cheeks created tiny little explosions as the air jumped from his mouth. Then as Sorenson left the kitchen and walked back through the dining room and finally into the dimly lighted front of the house, Jerky released the safety catch on the weapon. He watched as Sorenson's moves became strangely predictable, as though he were pacing through the house in a predetermined route. Jerky knew as he lay there that with one round from the rifle he would be able to take off Sorenson's head.

He never got the chance. The bulldozer seemed to settle on him in two stages, very close together. First, his ankles and knees were pinned to the ground, then a rush of water from the tipping bulldozer spilled across his back and legs. Digging his elbows into the ground as hard as he could, he tried with all his strength to pull himself forward. The ground under him was nothing but a light carpet over a thin mixture of water and soil. His elbows flipped two little divots behind him, and pure clear water rushed to fill the holes. The other end of the bulldozer dropped on him in a way that was both slow and fast, as if it were somehow enjoying itself. It rolled up his legs and onto the small of his back, and then in one final, evening-out effort it pressed him flat several inches into the ground. The few bubbles of air that escaped from his mouth and nose rested for a few moments along the top of the shiny surface water. Then one by one they made little pops and disappeared.

During the five days that the people in the town looked for Jerky, Sorenson bought out the Graftons, Woodmans, and a new family, the Lucarellis, who had only two years before moved to Oldenfield from Mattapan, Massachusetts. The three families had lived in the ugly, misshapen structures on the edge of town, and Sorenson got them all for just under twelve thousand. The four thousand each family was paid was the most money any of them had seen in a long time. They were big families, twenty-one in all of them put together, and the first thing they did with the money was to clean out Millie's beer cooler and then the reserve supply she kept in the basement. They bought eighteen cases, the eight loose six-packs in the cooler, and uncountable numbers of quart bottles. Millie did not speak to them the whole time they were in the store, even when several of the women asked if there had been word on Jerky.

Somehow in the town it had been assumed that Jerky had gone hunting on the mountain and was up there either lost or hurt or, as they assumed at nightfall on the third day, dead. "Something's happened," Millie said over and over again during those five days. "Something awful. I can smell it."

It was Sorenson who found Jerky. During the five days that he was missing, the weather turned very hot and dry, and following the rain a stiff southwesterly wind blew for three days. The bulldozer that had flattened Jerky into the ground seemed to rise up out of its ruts a few inches each day as the water dried up beneath it. As Sorenson was leaving his house very early on the morning of the fifth day, the sun reflected off Jerky's rifle and caught Sorenson square in the eyes. He walked across the lawn a little way, stopping short when he saw that what looked like loosely scattered clothes under the bulldozer really had Jerky's body in them.

Jerky was buried in one of the single plots that sat low in the knoll down near Route 10. There had been a very short service for him at the church, and the one at graveside was scarcely longer. Almost no one in the town came, and those who did showed up only because of Millie. Including Barker, only six people were at the burial: Moose, Culver and Ellen, and Simmer. All of them looked not only shocked, but afraid of something distant and undefinable.

Worst of all was Millie. She looked as if her soul were made up entirely of shattered cartilage. Her face sat a little into her head as though it had been beaten with a spiritual hammer. She stood relaxed in a defeated way, like a boxer who suddenly realizes that some minutes before someone has knocked him out. And Millie looked somehow smaller, her full square frame suddenly attacked by a smoldering age. She stood in her black dress and black hat like a grandmother who has suddenly run out of family. Occasionally, as Barker ran through the words of the service, Millie's mouth moved a little, as if she were uttering small prayers. Actually, she was cursing Jerky. "You bastard little kid," she breathed, so softly that no one was able to hear her. "Always you been no good." Every now and again her mouth moved over the words and pushed them out.

The heat had begun to rise very early that morning. A little after five Millie had watched the sun crank itself up behind a wet bluish haze that was almost like a vague, transparent curtain. The heat and dampness had not gone away during the night, had held themselves ready and awake through the darkness. The black flies and the big mosquitoes swam in the early morning air as though they were self-appointed escorts for the funeral, and they followed Millie and the others, first to the church and then on to the cemetery. All during Barker's words the bugs moved lazily among those standing by the open grave. Hands and arms moved in a polite slow motion as they brushed at the flies and mosquitoes. Moose and Culver had the most trouble with them. Moose's face was reddened as if he had been slapped, and Culver's neck was dotted with raised red welts from where the flies had bitten him.

Moose and Simmer walked away with Millie after Barker finished, and then Culver moved off to follow them. Barker took Ellen's arm as though to steady her, and then they too moved away from the grave. As they all walked up the path to the top of the knoll, it seemed as if the flies and mosquitoes made a conscious decision to stay where they were. There was a scrambled buzzing over the grave as though the bugs were for a moment very confused. But then a calm and a silence began to ease itself on the place, and the flies and mosquitoes settled like a thin blanket on the lid of the coffin.

Barker and Ellen drove back to the church in the station wagon they had used to bring Jerky's body to the cemetery, but the others walked the half mile back to the main part of town. As they walked, Moose tried to comfort Millie as best he could, and Simmer never took his arm from hers. But it seemed that with each step Millie grew stronger, and by the time they were in front of her store her body was fully erect, her head squared on her shoulders, her arms ready to throw off Simmer and Moose. The three of them stood for a few moments in the heat, the only sound an occasional black fly that hummed among them. Moose took out an old yellow handkerchief and wiped his forehead several times. Then he folded his arms and turned to Millie. "You be all right?" he asked. She nodded at him when he said, "You get some rest now."

"There's enough rest in work," she said.

"What're you going to do?"

"Open the store," she said. "And keep it open. This ain't a town right now, not with its store and post office shut up." She turned quickly to Simmer. "And your place," she added. She moved her hands in front of her as though to shoo the men away. "Let's get going," she said quietly; "let's get things open before that s.o.b. buys everything right out from under us." She turned away and went into the store.

Millie stood just inside the door for a few minutes and looked at the shelves and the thinned-out, dwindling stock they held. There were large holes where whole sections of food had been bought out and not replaced, and Millie thought for a moment that never would she have the strength to stack another row of cans or set the bags of flour and sugar in the places where they'd always gone. She started slowly down the narrow center aisle. Unconsciously she took off her hat, holding it in her hands like a large black saucer. Then her eyes began to fly over the stock. She calculated with great precision exactly what she would need to order the next week; then she subtracted the stock not yet shelved. When she passed the counter the first time she set her hat to one side and wrote down the number of cases of soup, beans, jellies, spices and so forth that she would order. Then her eyes swept the cases directly in front of the counter, and the bread and pastry orders tallied automatically in her mind. Just as she finished writing down those numbers, she seemed struck full in the back by some enormous weight, and she thought for an instant that she was going to fall flat across the counter. The whole panorama of the funeral and burial suddenly fell on her and in a rapid-fire sequence played out completely in her head. She steadied herself on the counter for a moment, and then her hands began to take little steps back toward her, and finally with a great effort she came fully erect again. After a moment when she seemed to be holding her breath, she said out loud, "I haven't cried in a hundred years." Then she whirled around and started for the beverage case.

That night after she had cleaned out Jerky's room, after she had packed all his belongings into boxes in the basement, and after she had finished two cans of beer, she cried for several hours. She did not so much cry as wail and moan, like a sad, grieving mountain.

Four

Just after the Fourth of July the population of Oldenfield was under forty. The houses Sorenson had taken stood empty and forlorn, almost as if they were people fully aware of being close to death. There was no pattern to the people who had sold out. The empty houses were sprinkled among the town at random, and the ugly worry of five months before had slid into a pure despair. Even though Sorenson now came and went in the town as though he had always been a part of it, and even though people moved out regularly, everything about the interstate was still a sick black theory. It was as if people were waiting for some force to come and overnight crush them and the town flat. But Sorenson's operation amounted to a kind of subtraction from the town, and he was content to take what he could in little bites and snatches. There were no more crises in the town, no more angry gatherings at Millie's store. Everyone simply knew that the whole town was being nibbled away, but even in that knowledge there was denial. It came in the form of Volunteer Day and whether in fact it should be held at all. Millie and Moose thought the whole idea was, as she put it, "pretty damn silly," but Simmer and Culver took the opposite view, and their authority persuaded the rest of those still left in the town. But it was a dismal effort, a sickening day.

As in years past, the long tables were set out on the wide lawn in front of town hall, set in rows that ran all the way down to the street. Ellen Thomas, as in the past, took charge of putting out the signs, and she did so with great care. The signs read: "Jams—Jellies," "Cakes—Pies," "Knitted Goods," "Books—Old, New," and "Leftovers." On the last one could be found anything and everything, from useless old glass bottles to clothes so out of date that they always brought giggles to the people who picked them over.

It was clear almost immediately that Volunteer Day was not going to raise money to maintain the fire truck, nor was it going to accomplish anything else except show those still in the town how severely their numbers had decreased. Spread out over nearly twenty-five tables were eight cakes, eleven pies, six jars of jam, one knitted bedspread, two boxes of books, and on the "Leftover" table, by itself, an old American flag, moth-eaten and severely faded, that had been folded into a tight military wedge. It had once belonged to Culver, but it had no sentimental value whatsoever. He had gotten it many years before on the same table on the same day.

Of the thirty-seven people in the town on Volunteer Day, not more than fifteen put in an appearance. Culver, Ellen and Simmer stayed most of the day, and Moose came out of the post office to talk with them when things were slack. When Millie closed her store at noon and came up to town hall, she found only Ellen sitting on a little aluminum lawn chair staring up the street toward her house. Millie picked through the jams and finally bought a cake, but when she gave Ellen the money they did not speak.

Along toward four o'clock Ellen and Culver cleaned off what was left on the tables and put it all in the back of his pickup. They folded and stacked the tables back in their places in the basement of town hall and then left. Culver took Ellen home first, and then he went straight to the dump, where with an old snow shovel he quickly pushed all the unbought things into a heap.

When Culver got home from the dump he found Ellen sitting in her rocking chair staring into the cold black fireplace in the living room. When he came up to her she spoke quickly, before he had a chance to assess the deathlike expression on her face. "I want to go to Mother's house in Newfield," she said.

"Just like that?" Culver said. He snapped his fingers like a rifle shot. "You quit just like that?"

"I want to go home."

"You're weak."

"I know that," she said quietly.

"This is my home," Culver announced to the room.

"Mr. Barker has asked me to sing in the Newfield church in August," she said.

"I don't give a goddamn," Culver said.

"I could get Mother's house ready," she said.

"No," Culver roared, "you will not go. We will stay here and fight this thing down to the last person, the last house."

"Why?" Ellen asked. Culver's eyes began to dart furiously around the room, as though he might find the answer to Ellen's question in one of the dark corners. Finally he looked squarely at her and said, "Because of what I would be to myself if I didn't."

"August first," she said.

The heavy thick heat that settled on the town during the week of Jerky's funeral was the first real bad spell of weather that summer. The second came a little after the middle of July and stayed for almost ten days. Then suddenly one afternoon a line of weather swept through the town and seemed to scrub the air to a high polish. There were fierce thunderstorms and a great deal of lightning, but very little rain. The wind swirled and beat upon everything in gusts of controlled fury. The late afternoon sun all but disappeared for nearly an hour, but when the front finally passed, it left things fresher than they had been in early spring, somehow more turgid and greener than they ever should have been.

Simmer knew that evening as he sat outside his gas station that even though it was not yet the end of July, the high leaves in some of the older trees would be coloring around their edges within two or three days. When August first came two days later, he hardly had to look up from his work to know that he was right. But it was not the kind of change that anyone could really yet see. What Simmer experienced that morning was more of a feeling to the air, almost a hard twinge somewhere in the inner regions of the soul.

The first and only person to come to the gas station that morning was Calvin Runners. Since the town meeting in March, Runners had grown fatter, and he was now to the point where it was difficult for him to get out of his car, and he was short of breath all the time. When he tried to tell Simmer that a crew of men was roaming freely through the town, he sputtered and gasped pathetically.

"How many?" Simmer asked patiently.

"Ten, twelve," Runners said in two little bursts of air from the very front of his mouth.

"That'll be the rodmen," Simmer said, as though to himself. He thought for a moment, while Runners stood like a lieutenant awaiting directions. "Any heavy machinery?"

"Nobody said nothing."

"It's the surveyors," Simmer said. "And you can wager Sorenson's not far behind."

"He's there," Runners blurted. "He's telling them everything to do."

"It's time somebody laid the bastard in the street." Simmer's face drained itself of any discernible age, and almost instantly there was a freshness to him that startled even Runners. He moved quickly the twenty or so yards to his pickup, and then with one foot on the short square step he went rigid as if he'd been shot. What stopped him so violently was the distant muffled roar of dynamite. He stood fixed where he was, every hair on his body suddenly a little antenna, and then he slumped a little when the sound of the second explosion vaulted the mountain and slid like an avalanche into the deepest parts of the valley.

As if he suddenly understood everything that was happening, he got into the truck and, without so much as a glance at Runners, started off down Route 10. As he drove he expected to find the heavy machinery and the construction teams just around each turn in the road. Then in a silent calculation he knew he had judged wrong. The explosions had seemed to him not more than a quarter of a mile away, but as he drove on he realized that he had badly misjudged their intensity. As he clocked off the mileage he became almost panicky, and when he saw that he had come three miles he muttered to himself, "What in God's name are they using?"

It was another three miles before Simmer came over a little rise in the road. He looked out toward a heavily wooded section several hundred yards off the road and saw a swath of pure space where most of the woods had stood. Even at this distance he could see where small clumps of dirt had rained down on the road. Simmer eased the truck to the side of the road and sat in the cab like a small bewildered animal. He stared for a long time at the huge space in the woods. It looked to him awkward and brutal. For a moment he looked away from it, his eyes sweeping the solid line of trees farther down the horizon. When he looked back, he saw the space as permanent and highly organized, rugged and defiant in its own right; but what amazed him now was its breadth. The space dominated the whole near horizon, and where the long thin line of trees had run evenly against the sky, there was now only space that appeared capable of multiplying itself. Simmer saw it for a moment as a great mouth eating its way through the countryside, swallowing everything in its path, and he felt a kind of red fear race through him. Then in the next few minutes it was as though he had been given a special knowledge, and his whole body rose up out of the seat and pressed forward against the steering wheel. It was as if he were trying to get closer to the space, to study hard the little trucks and small bulldozers that crawled back and forth like so many mechanical insects. His mind searched for some way he could stop them all, and just as he had decided that the machinery in the distance was in fact stoppable, he saw, coming up over the horizon line, the largest bulldozer he had ever seen. Even from his distance of several hundred yards, Simmer could see that the bulldozer was at least two or three stories tall. Its blade jutted in front of it like the wet dripping prow of a ship, like two great wings suddenly unfolded for flight. As he sat there, he knew that he would never be able to describe the sight to anyone.

Suddenly from the distance he heard the high shrill sound of the warning whistle, and he knew that the men dotting the horizon were readying another charge of dynamite. He watched for another few moments as the machines crawled over the little thin line and sank down behind it. Then he started his truck, turned it in a smooth U, and slowly started the drive back to Oldenfield. He heard the explosion roll out of the ground and chatter along the hills, and for just an instant it seemed to pick up the truck and hurtle it along the road. Then it began to die out quietly in the distance far ahead of him.

All along the road back to Oldenfield, Simmer saw where the surveyors had done their work. Tall stakes jutted up in the fields and by the side of the road, so that it looked as if the path for the interstate had been there perfectly disguised for longer than anything else and was only now beginning to show itself. Route 10 wound around the right-of-way in a lazy fashion, in some places departing from it to seek its own old way around the hills. When that happened Simmer could see where the right-of-way shot straight ahead, where the stakes pounded away from Route 10 and, like an invisible carpet not yet put down, headed arrogantly for the hills in its path. And as if they had somehow been there all along, Simmer saw the rodmen and surveyors come out from the woods in twos and threes, their equipment slung over their shoulders like so many funny-looking rifles. For just an instant Simmer thought that the fluorescent orange of the pullovers made them look like inviting targets.

Sorenson had not been in the town much during the last part of June and almost all of July, and as usual when he was not there people in the town did not even think about him. But when he did come, and especially when he stayed for several days, the townspeople acted like a colony of disturbed insects. Those who had turned down Sorenson's first offers on their houses and land were the most upset. When his Chevrolet was parked anywhere in town they drove past it slowly, and when he was in the post office or store people stayed longer than they needed to. They half-wanted the chance to tell him no once more, and half-wanted to know how much lower his next offer would be. They acted like sad, defeated gamblers waiting for the wheel to stop and tell them for sure how much they had lost.

But when Sorenson came back on August first and more or less led the surveyors through town as though he were a platoon leader, he was visibly changed. He looked, in fact, like a man who with enormous effort has gotten out of a sickbed. Those in the town who saw him that morning stood still and studied him. He was thinner and somehow straighter-looking. His eyes were hollowed out like a sick man's, but there was a brightness and clarity to them, as though he had undergone some purification that even he did not understand.

With a huge map laid out over the tailgate of the station wagon, Sorenson directed the surveyors to the places just outside the town where they could pick up the easterly points of the right-of-way. Then in two small all-terrain vehicles, which really looked like enormous toys, the men loaded their transits and huge expandable rods and went off into the woods. Sorenson stood in the middle of the street and watched until the vehicles were around the bend by Simmer's Garage. Then he turned and began to walk slowly toward the post office.

In the past two weeks his headaches had been a good deal more brief and less intense than they had all summer, and his relief showed clearly on his face. He looked like a man given new life. The headaches had started slowly, almost as a gentle tapping at the top of his neck, but very quickly they had established a pattern of their own. After a few weeks of trying to get inside his skull, they seemed to suddenly one day make the leap from the very top of his neck to just inside the lowest curvature of the skull bones. For weeks they sat there as if unsure where to go, and Sorenson was never really free from a dull, low throbbing. But it was the sort of pain that one could live with, and after a month of easy, steady pounding he rarely thought about it. He had no trouble sleeping, and it was not until just after his breakfast each morning that the quiet rumbling began in the back of his head.

However, two weeks before he had started the paper work on the right-of-way the headaches had suddenly worsened. Like two small powerful arms they had started at the base of his skull and now were spread out along the inside circumference of his whole head. When the lines of pain met between his eyes, a great pressure was perfectly distributed throughout his whole head. He went to a whole string of doctors, each of whom told him something different. One said he was simply over-worked, another that he probably needed bifocals; a third, an older sickly man himself, said flatly that Sorenson needed to get married. Finally, through his office with the state, Sorenson saw a specialist in Boston who, after a thorough and extensive examination, declared there was nothing wrong with Sorenson. The specialist gave him prescriptions for Librium and Darvon, but Sorenson threw away the pills after the first day because they dulled his senses and made him suspect error in every calculation he made. He decided that he would simply have to live with the pain, and with that decision came a lessening of the discomfort during the day and a huge increase of it at night. The pain was so intense that for months Sorenson was able to do nothing at night, and the only way he kept sane was to pace through Mrs. Keller's house in a great circular path. Often he thought that it would have been a blessing if Jerky Barnhope had blown his head off.

When Sorenson got to the post office that morning, there was an unusual number of townspeople milling around. Those who had come early to collect their mail had stayed, talking in little groups and watching the sur-veyors and rodmen begin their work. The little clusters of people in front of the door of the post office separated and flattened themselves against the side of the building as Sorenson went past them. In the months before, when he had come to the post office, people had tossed remarks at him, and some had even tried to brush by him hard, as if to catch a shoulder or in some way hurt him. Now, though, there was almost the feeling that he carried some fearful disease and that the townspeople knew to keep their distance.

Sorenson went directly to the window and asked Moose if there was mail for him. Moose produced a pile of letters and several official-looking envelopes, all neatly held together by two thick rubber bands. "You got to sign for the bottom three Certifieds," Moose said, sliding the little yellow receipts out of the window. Sorenson signed them all by making a large *S,* followed by a hard straight line that ran right off the paper.

As he turned to leave, Simmer burst through the open door and stood directly in his way. In a voice that carried well out into the street he said, "There's some of us just never going to move. You know that."

"There always are," Sorenson answered. His voice sounded light but tired, as if he did not wish to say more.

"How are you going to do it?" Simmer shouted. "Are we just plowed under like last year's fields?" The people outside had crowded closer to the door to hear what Simmer was saying, and the last remark was addressed more to them than to Sorenson.

"In a town like this we'd probably need the wrecking ball for a half day. Can't see as it'd be much more." Sorenson answered as though he were reporting ball scores.

"What do you do with the *people?*" Simmer said directly. He brought his fists to his hips and let them rest there. *"Us!"*

"If you're still here the day we blade off, then I go and get a court order to have you removed. With the court order comes the sheriff," Sorenson went on quietly, "and if you don't go peaceably, then the state troopers come within an hour or so and"—he paused as if he'd planned it all along, and his face curled a little as if he were tired of toying with Simmer—"and then we drag your collective asses into the street," he said slowly and viciously.

The two men looked at each other just long enough for the people outside to worry that things would directly come to blows. Finally Simmer said, "You love it, don't you?"

"It's a job," Sorenson answered carefully. His eyes swept Simmer's face as if he were suddenly a little afraid of him.

"You really love it," Simmer said again. In his voice there was the hint that he suddenly understood Sorenson.

"And what precisely is it that I love?"

"Destruction," Simmer said quickly.

"November fifteenth is when you'll all be gone," Sorenson said.

Simmer suddenly looked a little stupid, and for the first time he looked away from Sorenson, his eyes wandering all over the inside of the post office. "You can't make six miles in three and a half months," he finally said.

"The road is as the crow flies," Sorenson said. "Two miles now, give or take a rod or two." He looked past Simmer and out to the people standing by the front door. He smiled at them in a sweet, sickening way and then looked back to Simmer. Quietly he said, "Now you get the hell out of my way."

As Sorenson went by, Simmer whispered, "Somebody ought to cut you into little pieces."

"Better than you have tried," Sorenson answered without looking back.

Following him out the door, Simmer stood on the top step and watched him walk down toward Mrs. Keller's house. "You won't make November fifteenth," he shouted after him. Sorenson never looked back, and when after a few moments Simmer turned back to face the townspeople, they did not look at him. In twos and threes they seemed to slide away from the post office without really moving, and in a few more minutes the whole little crowd was gone.

When Ellen Thomas said she was leaving August first, she was as good as her word. When Culver got back from the post office that morning, he was eager to tell Ellen how Simmer had put it to Sorenson, how he had shut him up in front of everyone in the town. But he never got the chance. As he came up the street he saw one of the trucks from the Niles Construction Company parked in front of his house. He slowed his walk almost to a slow-motion creep as he watched Ellen's belongings go into the truck. The three men were quick and efficient, and Culver stopped and watched them from some yards off. The truck was backed almost to the front door of the house, its rear looking like a huge mouth about to engulf the front door.

Suddenly things became too much for Culver, and his whole body slumped so that he had to reach out to a tree for support. When he was finally able to control himself, he pushed off from the tree and walked toward the house like a man who has suddenly aged ten years. His chest and belly sagged as with a great weight; his backbone became slack and fibrous, and he was suddenly aware that his knees would not straighten as he walked. With the slow, even gait of a man who clearly has no purpose, he went straight past the truck and into the living room. He sat in his easy chair by the window, the mail still held loosely in one hand.

When Ellen came into the room, she was guiding two men who were carrying a bird's-eye maple dresser. She barely glanced at Culver as she stepped aside and allowed the men to walk the dresser through the room and directly into the truck.

Culver flipped the mail into his lap and looked at her. "I'll not sell," he said.

"Suit yourself," Ellen said, as though all along it had been decided. As Culver watched another dresser go by, he suddenly felt a crushing wave of grief for the whole town. It flushed through his body and then settled visibly onto his face like a rising wave of nausea.

"When you need me," she said.

Culver waved his hand in front of him, and it stopped open, as if she were meant to read an answer scribbled in his palm. "I'll not sell," he said.

Culver sat where he was for a long time after Ellen left. In fact, several hours later he was not even sure when she had gone. He became aware only that a vast and treacherous loneliness had suddenly invaded the house, as if it were a person able to stalk many rooms at once.

It was not until the sun was framed in the west windows of the living room that Culver finally got out of the chair and went into the kitchen. He looked around for a few minutes, as though he were in a strange place. Finally he realized that Ellen had left him enough dishes and utensils to get along. He went to the cupboard over the stove, and taking out a can of tuna fish, he opened it with an old hand opener and tossed the ragged top into the garbage. He began to eat from the can with his fingers, picking out the larger chunks easily, then licking at the smaller shreds that stuck to his fingers.

As he ate, he looked out over the fields and pastures in the back, and then his gaze swept over the land in the distance near the tree line at the beginning of the mountain. He stared for a long time, as though watching something afar off. Finally, Culver saw the soft black outline of his dog moving at a very fast pace across the high field. As if fleeing from something terrifying, the huge strong animal took two stone boundary fences simply by lengthening his stride a little. It wasn't until he was over the fence a couple of hundred yards from the house that Culver noticed that he was carrying something in his mouth. He put down the can of tuna fish and leaned closer to the window. "God damn," he said in enormous admiration. He picked up the can and drank the oil from it, then dropped the can in the garbage sack by the back door and went out quickly to the little porch.

The dog's gait was slower, as if he had eased off as he drew closer to the house. He walked the last thirty yards with his black head held high, the prize in his mouth gripped with a firm tenderness. His long black tail swept the air behind him in rhythm with his strides. His muscles quivered all over from both the run and the pride he obviously felt over his catch. Culver watched carefully as the dog came up to him on the porch, whirled and heeled in glee, and then dropped his catch directly at Culver's feet.

It was the heart of a deer.

"My Christ," Culver said to the dog, "I didn't need this today."

He ordered the dog to stay, then went into the house; when he came back out he was loading his .22 rifle. The dog followed him down off the porch and stood in front of him. Obviously excited by the presence of the rifle, he made a couple of dashing motions toward the field, as if to encourage Culver to hurry, but when Culver commanded him to sit, he did so immediately. The dog watched as Culver carefully put the end of the barrel against the soft black fur between his eyes and pulled the trigger. For an instant it appeared that the dog would continue to sit there forever, that he would always hold his tight obedient position, that he would always be looking up the barrel. But then as if taken by a giant crushing wind, he flipped back and away from Culver several feet and lay still on the grass.

Culver buried the dog in a shallow grave just on the far side of the boundary fence, and it was just past sunset when he was finished. On the way back to the house he shot three crows sitting together on the branch of a dead maple tree at the far end of the pasture. He got the first one easily, the second as it leaped in flight from the branch, and the third a couple of seconds later as it flew in bewilderment directly toward him.

The next morning Sorenson was at the post office a good twenty minutes before Moose came down to open up. He had not slept much during the night, partly from work and partly from the pain of his headaches, and it was with great relief that he had watched the sun come up. Dawn somehow washed the throbbing from his head, somehow cleaned out his body. He had listened carefully to the thousands of birds throughout the town as they had first awakened, and in a strange way Sorenson had fancied himself in control of them all. He stood in his living room looking out on the street, all the windows of the downstairs thrown open as if in invitation, and as soon as he heard the first chirping he raised a forefinger and almost began to conduct the sounds as they quickly multiplied. The headache he had endured had left all of his senses infinitely sharper, as though the pain had been able to refine his hearing, sight and smell to a high degree of perception. The first few minutes of the birds' singing were pleasant and clear, but as the sounds of the morning gathered together they created a fierce momentum in his head, and finally it seemed to Sorenson that each bird had tuned itself perfectly to an individual cell in his brain, and he felt for a few seconds as though his head would explode. Quickly he closed all the windows and went into the kitchen in the back of the house. He made some toast and drank some water with it, and then he gathered the thirty-two envelopes he had worked on throughout the night and checked the figures in them one last time.

When Moose finally opened up, Sorenson carried the envelopes past him and set them down in a little pile in front of Moose's window. "You'd want?" Moose said as he came around through the back and stopped at the window.

"Fifty regulars," Sorenson said. He put a creased five-dollar bill on the counter.

"I didn't know you had fifty friends," Moose said.

"You can bet I don't," Sorenson said in a very strong voice.

Moose slid the stamps to him and in the same motion took the money. Turning away, Sorenson went to the narrow high table by the window. With great care he began to separate individual stamps from the sheet Moose had given him, working at it much like a child engrossed in a new toy. When he was finished, the stamps lay on the table like the pieces of a simple puzzle, and Sorenson methodically began to wet each one with spit from his lower lip. For some reason he was inept at what he did, as though suddenly his hands had decided on their own that they would not work properly. The stamps went on the envelopes in crooked and sloppy ways, sometimes half of one hanging off the corner of the envelope. Sorenson actually glued several stamps half to the envelope and half to the table itself. But what was truly ugly about the whole procedure was Sorenson's inability to control the saliva in his mouth, and most of the stamps ended up sitting loosely on the corner of the envelope almost floating on a little ball of spit.

It took Sorenson a long time to stamp the envelopes, and when he was finished he looked as if he had put in a full day's work. He handed the envelopes to Moose with obvious pride, and Moose held them for a moment as if weighing them. Then quickly his fingers began to sort through them, but before he was more than a third through he stopped and looked at Sorenson. "They're all for the town?" he said. Sorenson nodded to him. "And to save me the trouble," Moose went on, "what might they be?"

"Offers," Sorenson answered. "Final, non-negotiable."

"And what do you have in store for me?" Moose asked. He held the envelopes as though they were a large deck of cards.

"Thirty-nine five," Sorenson answered; then he added, "I'm going to look very good when this is all over."

"There'll be some you'll never buy out," Moose said. "There'll be some you'll have to drag into the street."

"Who?" Sorenson asked eagerly.

"Those who got nowhere else to go," Moose answered. He lifted his eyes and looked beyond Sorenson to the empty street bathed in the early morning sunlight. He seemed for a moment to be remembering some magnificent personal event. "Those who ain't got nobody," he said. Then almost instantly his eyes flashed back to Sorenson and he said, "Next time you dump a load like this here, you put them in strict alphabetical order."

"The trouble with you people is you don't reason," Sorenson said.

"But we do," Moose answered. He turned away and with quick short motions of his right arm began to deal the envelopes into their boxes. Then in mid-motion he suddenly stopped and turned back to Sorenson. "I'd bet you that before this is over, somebody is going to lay open your head."

"One thing you do not do is threaten me," Sorenson suddenly yelled at Moose. His voice exploded through the room, and he smashed his fist on the little table at the window. "Nobody threatens me." His eyes were wide in an anger that had burst out of an infinite black hole in him. It was as if the whole world had always threatened him and that finally he was striking back at it. "That crazy deranged kid with his goddamn rifle," Sorenson said. "He actually tried to kill me—you know that?"

"Only good idea the boy ever had," Moose said. He resumed his sorting of the envelopes, and even when the front door crashed shut after Sorenson, Moose took no notice of it.

Sorenson went straight to Millie's store, where his greeting was far less cordial than Moose's had been. Sorenson wanted to tell Millie that the figure he had given on her property was actually twice what the property was worth, and that he hoped she would understand the overpayment to be in some way compensation for the loss of her son. He hardly got the chance to open his mouth. As he stepped inside the door, Millie brought up from under the counter the rifle Jerky had tried to use on him, pointing it straight at him. "You'd make a hell of a mess this close up," she said, sighting along the barrel.

Sorenson, his face suddenly ghost-white and so slack that it seemed it would peel off and drop to the floor, leaned back against the door jamb as though to wait for her to shoot. Finally, looking over at the collection of soup cans to his right, he said, "I've come about my final offer."

"I can't tell you what thrills I get from that."

"Will you put down that thing?" he asked as he turned slightly toward her.

"I could put four bullets in you before you hit the floor," she said. She held her position as if she had been frozen into it. "Now you say what you have to and then get the hell out of here."

"I made the offer seventy-two nine," he said. His eyes flipped from the soup cans just in time to catch Millie's first expression as the figure registered with her. She looked as if some magnificent super-soft bullet had hit her in the middle of the forehead. Sorenson watched as the effects spread in a kind of dazzling slow-motion across the rest of her face. Her body seemed to lose its sturdiness and its rigidity, and for a second or two it seemed to Sorenson that every hard line of her frame rippled a little, then became jellylike and fluid. As if it were suddenly just plain too heavy for her, the rifle dropped slowly from her hands and rested on the counter. Millie never took her eyes from Sorenson.

"Two questions," she said. Her voice suddenly sounded neutered; it was metallic and distant, a thing to carry information. "Where do you get money like that?"

"You people are such damned fools," he answered. Now for the first time he turned full toward her, but he did not move any closer. "You nickel-and-dime your lives. You know nothing about money. You and a lot of other people could have gotten a lot of money from this little misadventure, an awful lot of money."

"Where do you get money like seventy-two thousand dollars?" Millie asked again, as if she had not heard him.

"My allocation for the town was a little over a million three," he said. Then he added, "I haven't spent even half of it."

"I make maybe six, seven thousand in a good year." Her voice seemed to be losing its direction, as though she had suddenly started a conversation with herself.

"Question two," Sorenson said. He folded his arms across his chest and with open arrogance leaned casually back against the wall.

"Why so much for a store?"

"It's about right," he said.

"I'm dumb, I know that," Millie answered, "but give me credit for at least being able to count."

"You've got river frontage," Sorenson said. "It's got to count for something."

"Come on," she said, "that's barely a stream out there."

"There's an acre or so in the back," he said.

"Hardly."

"It's a fair price," he told her.

"It's because of my boy."

"It is," Sorenson said slowly. He pushed himself away from the door jamb and leaned against the ends of the shelves. Looking down, he rubbed his forefinger through the dust on the top of a fat can of stew. "Business pretty poor?" he said indifferently.

"There isn't any business," Millie said.

"Your boy was a very upset young man," Sorenson tossed at her, "even a little disturbed. Did he use drugs?"

"You got any kids?"

"No, thank you," Sorenson answered. He waved his hand a little in front of his face as though saying good-bye and grinned childishly at Millie.

"When you've had a kid, and when he gets to be twenty-three or so," Millie said in an even voice, "and when you're done with burying him, then you come back and we'll talk some more about it."

Each of them seemed once again to harden up, to go rigid somewhere very deep inside, and Millie rotated the rifle on the counter so that as it lay on its side it pointed again at Sorenson.

"You'll accept the seventy-two nine?" Sorenson asked. He moved back a little from the shelves to the door.

"That will be hard to turn down," she said.

"You realize, of course, that you can't tell anyone you're getting that much." Sorenson leaned over and picked up the can of stew and casually held it in his hand. He studied the label for a few seconds. "Until this is all over, of course," he added.

"It would have to be our little secret," Millie said. Sorenson smiled at her, and then with a great satisfied grin on his face he nodded. "Hold up the can," Millie said. Sorenson looked at her and then at the can in his left hand. Almost instinctively he held it up and away from him. Millie picked up the rifle from the counter, and as Sorenson watched in horror she carefully brought it to her shoulder. "Now bearing in mind," she said, "that the can is about the size of your heart . . ."

"No," Sorenson breathed, his face and body suddenly shaking in tightly controlled waves. "For God's . . ." he started to say.

"Now bearing in mind . . ." Millie said again, and then she pulled the trigger. The roar of the gunshot in the store was almost unbelievable. The building seemed to throb for many minutes as it made an almost conscious effort to contain the explosion. A good portion of the lighter merchandise—the cracker boxes, the tobacco pouches—flew off the counters, and several unstable shelves slid all their contents onto the floor. Sorenson's hand was still up and away from him, half open as though holding the can of stew. But the can was gone, as was the front-door glass. Bits of meat, potatoes and carrots were imbedded in the old dry wood around the door and its frame. Some of the pieces looked as if they had been beaten into the wood with a hammer. The meat in places was almost white, the carrots and other vegetables so deeply rammed in that they had taken on the color of the stain in the wood. In a way that quite surprised her, Millie felt as shaken and frightened as Sorenson. But she did not show it. With her head tilted ever so slightly to one side she put the rifle down without taking her eyes from Sorenson. The air all around her held the bitter bright taste of the gunshot, and Millie knew that if she breathed deeply she would cough. The two of them stared at each other for what seemed a very long time, and then Sorenson began to shake all over, Millie watching in horror as he stood with a kind of absurd helplessness. Finally, after a few more minutes, she said, "Are you all right?"

"Oh, no, no," he said as though to someone else in the store, and then, a little hunched over and still shaking hard, he turned and pushed open the door and bolted outside.

"You son of a bitch," Millie called after him, but her voice barely carried to the canned-goods case near the door where Sorenson had stood. Her mouth seemed to be winding down as if it belonged to a worn and twisted doll. She reeled just a little and sat so hard in the lawn chair behind the register that three of the plastic strips snapped. But the chair did not give way, and Millie sat motionless, watching the blue cloud from the gunshot settle above the shelves as though it were now permanent.

The morning before, when Sorenson had pretty much destroyed Simmer at the post office, was one of the worst and strangest in all of Simmer's life. As the townspeople had wandered away, some to their homes, some to follow Sorenson to talk about his offers, Simmer's vision suddenly blurred and doubled slightly, so that for a few minutes he stood outside the post office rubbing his eyes and blinking hard. After a few more minutes he began to see the people walking after Sorenson as if they were many hundreds of yards away. They looked small to him, suddenly shrunk down to toy size by his own eyes. But only the people were distorted in his vision; the trees and lawns along the street were as normal and lovely as they had always been—even, Simmer thought, somewhat more sharply outlined than he had ever noticed them.

Without really thinking about it, Simmer stepped off the little porch in front of the post office and began to walk slowly down the main street. In a way he wished that he could somehow catch up with the people following Sorenson, somehow start a fresh challenge to him that would be utterly final and decisive, but as the people followed Sorenson up the front walk to his house, Simmer kept going on down the road at his own slow, wandering pace. When he was no more than ten feet beyond the walk, he had already forgotten all about Sorenson and all about what a fool he had been to challenge him at the post office. In a very few seconds all of that was many years into his past, and the only hard reality that Simmer could trust was made up of the trees that seemed in an instant's compression of time to grow hundreds of feet taller, to loom up over the houses of the town in a warm, comforting arch.

He remembered when the trees that now shaded most of the houses were little more than saplings reaching only just past the first-story windows. He saw the houses along the street as they had been during World War I, scrubbed to a high luster, wirebrushed and painted bright whites and greens. And the street had teemed with activity then. The first few motor cars in the town proudly chugged up and down the main street, and Simmer remembered being with Jed Thompson when he brought the first car in from Newfield. It had taken nearly an hour to cover the rutted five miles, but when they had finally reached the town, there had been a vast celebration.

As he walked, a thin private smile creased his reddish face as he remembered the winters before there had been snowplows. The townspeople who had motor cars put them up on blocks wherever they could find space, and the year that he had rented out his barn to six of the town cars was the unofficial beginning of Simmer's Garage. That winter he took apart every car in the barn and reassembled it, and when he did not know the name of a part, or could not find it out, he called it by one of the names of the townspeople, and until several years after the automatic transmission was introduced nearly everyone in the town had a part named after him. He thought back over them: the Buddy Collins part, the Sara Wright Jenkins part, the Talbot Todd part, and so on.

The winter Simmer worked on the cars was also the winter he sold his snow-rolling franchise in the town, and now as he walked past Millie's store he could see in his mind the great stallions just down near the end of the road, their nostrils fuming like steam hoses, sweat in white salt streaks across their shoulders and flanks. Behind them, the huge weighted rollers, their spikes caked with snow and ice, sat restless. And Simmer could see young Barton James struggling with his team from behind the rollers, whipping the air around them, hollering and swearing; finally the horses, in one last effort, dug into the waist-deep snow and were off, the rollers spinning behind them, snow flung all about, the harsh crunching sound everywhere slicing the morning air. And always within an hour after the rollers had done their work, the sleighs were out about the town, trade flourished, the people came and went as if they had jumped off a perfectly painted Christmas card. As Simmer got nearer the bend that led to his garage, he realized in a fleeting kind of way, almost as if it were a scent he was getting, that things had not really changed in the town, that he had preserved the ways of the people, that he almost singlehandedly had continued to roll the snow each winter, to paint the houses faithfully, to replace with care and precision every broken Buddy Collins part.

And, too, he remembered the winter mornings when he had awakened to see that the gray line of snow had risen to the middle of his bedroom window, when there was a hush that seemed to start from somewhere inside the house and spread itself out across the yards and the whole town. It seemed at those times that there was an immortality about him, a permanence to the house and town made certain by the weight of snow that held them all forever where they were. Always the cold followed the snow and froze it still and hard underfoot, so that when he walked to the barn it sounded as if he were walking on crushed glass.

Suddenly he was standing near the gas pumps in front of his garage, and all the warm nostalgic bubbles in him collectively went snap. He looked around for a long time and then walked over to the pumps. He stood between them, his arms outstretched, a hand lying softly across each of their rounded tops, and stared at the building in front of him. What had once pleased him enormously, had given meaning to himself and the town, now looked sick and ugly, a clapboard structure that looked as if a good stiff breeze would tumble it to the ground. Every flaw in the building magnified itself to Simmer and he was unable to see anything but a vast, warped, out-of-date building that had disease in every timber. Finally, when he could no longer bear to look at the building, he turned and took the hose from the gas pump on his right, and then the one on his left. He pulled them from their rollers, and when they were fully extended he began to walk toward the building. He held the nozzles out like exotic six-guns, as if he had suddenly decided to shoot it out with the building. Then he pressed off the release bars. The gasoline sprang from the hoses in long brownish streams, arched up and away from Simmer, and then splashed in continual fury halfway to the building. Simmer pulled the hoses out from the pumps, and when they would extend no further, he held them up around his shoulders in an effort to make the gasoline reach the building. In a rhythmic motion he tried to whip the nozzles as if to throw the gasoline. This gained him only about five feet, and finally he brought the nozzles back down to his hips and held them there while the gasoline flowed out. He watched as the liquid puddled, some of it working its way toward the foundation of the building. But most of the gasoline took the grade of the service area and began to roll back away from the building and toward Simmer. In a few minutes it was past him, then past the pumps, and finally after a little while it seeped into the sand by the side of the road twenty or so yards from the entrance to the service area.

Simmer did not hear Calvin Runners's truck as it pulled to a hard stop near the area where the gasoline trickle was running out of strength. Nor did he hear Runners's shouts at him. It was not until Runners was nearly on him that he turned just slightly from the hoses and saw him. He half-smiled and turned back to watch the gasoline. "For the love of all that's good and holy," Runners yelled, "what in hell's name are you doing?"

"Cleaning my nails," Simmer said.

"Are you crazy?"

"It's my station," Simmer said. "I can burn it down if I want to."

"Turn off the gas!" Runners yelled. Simmer looked at him for just an instant and smiled in a private way. Then Runners turned and ran the few yards to the office, and without even going inside he reached around the door and flipped off the switch box that controlled the electricity to the pumps. Instantly Simmer's hoses went dry and slack in his hands. He pumped with his hands, as if through his own rage he could make the gasoline again burst forward, and then he stood and watched Runners as he darted inside the garage and almost immediately came back out with a hose running clear water.

There was a tremendous amount of gasoline over the whole area, and Runners's first efforts to clear it from the asphalt got him nowhere. The water mixed with the gasoline, and then for a moment was captured by it in small pockets. But after a few more moments the hard current from the hose began to dilute the gasoline, and as it swept it past the pumps the heavy sweet-sour smell of the fumes began to lift. Runners swept the whole area in a careful rhythm, the water from the hose a kind of eerie snake, and as he did so he gazed at Simmer, who looked like an absurd defeated cowboy as he stood with the gasoline hoses dangling at his sides. "Put them up," Runners told him.

Simmer looked at him for a second or two and then turned and went to the pumps. He put the hoses back in place and turned to Runners. "I would have, you know."

"I wouldn't be proud of it," Runners said.

"You can go to hell."

"With the way the wind's up, you could have burned down the whole town," Runners said. "Would you want that?"

"It'd be better than letting him have it." The stream of water swept the asphalt near Simmer's feet, and he watched the water and gasoline fly up in little drops and stain his overalls. "I really would have done it," he said again. He looked at Runners and his face seemed shattered, as if his soul had suddenly been dumped onto it for all to see. His eyes seemed to sink more deeply into his head, the skin on his face was gray and cracked, and his mouth looked as if it had suddenly been shoved back into his jaws.

Runners turned the nozzle of the hose down to half strength and walked slowly over to the pumps. He held the hose out and away from him, the water coming from it in a fan-shaped spray. "You all right?" he asked.

"You remember how it was when they came home from the First War?" Simmer said. "A lot of them didn't get back until the late spring; some even came in the summer. Remember the band always being at the ready? We'd get off from school and go down to the depot and wave the flags for the guys coming in."

"So what?"

"Things meant something then." Simmer's eyes were distant and cool, with a detachment that was frightening to Runners. It was as if everything behind his eyes had suddenly turned to cement. "I've got to do something to him," Simmer said. Runners turned the nozzle of the hose so that the water ran from it in a hard little stream. "I mean it," Simmer said. His whole face suddenly became a red ash. "Goddamnit, do you think I don't?"

Runners stepped a little closer to him and raised one hand to touch a shoulder. "There's nothing left to do," he told Simmer.

"You're a woman, that's what you are. You act like one, you think like one."

"All right, all right," Runners said. He stepped back from Simmer and played the hose around the edge of the building in an angry way. Without looking up from the hose, he called out as Simmer walked away from the pumps, "Where you going?"

"To eat."

"Now? With the place like this?"

"It's eleven thirty-five," Simmer answered as he got to the door. "That's when I eat."

Simmer looked old only after a meal. The food settling into him had a warm and satisfying effect, and it seemed to spread itself throughout his body as if it were supplying a need beyond that which it served. His age seemed almost to double just after he finished eating. The erect quality of his body deteriorated almost instantly, and the sharp hard lines of his face melted into gentle folds. His eyes lost their focus, became watery and slow, and in their own independent way automatically prepared themselves for sleep. Always his lunchtime routine was the same: a bowl of tomato soup and a plain cheese sandwich, followed immediately by no more than a ten-minute nap at the table. Then, as he did every day, he went to the sink in the small kitchen and took out his teeth, washed them carefully, and then with a soft sucking sound put them back in his mouth.

When he got back outside, Runners had gone. The hose was still running, the water from it still washing over the whole area. In some places the asphalt was already crumbling a little and slick from the gasoline, and in other places the gasoline had worked its way into the cracks in the paving and had already started hundreds of little eruptions. It looked as if dozens of toy volcanoes were simultaneously trying to thrust themselves up through the asphalt, and in one or two spots Simmer was certain that he saw a couple of whiffs of steam. He knew that probably by the evening, certainly by the following morning, most of the area would be so heavily eroded and pocked that he wouldn't be able to walk on it.

Simmer turned away from the garage and looked out toward the woods and the gentle downslope of the mountain in the distance. For a few moments he seemed to be listening to some private sound. His head moved ever so slightly from one side to the other, and then turned a little more, as if he had finally understood what he heard. The air of the August afternoon surrounded him like a kind of perfect anesthetic. It was so pure that it seemed not to be there at all. It seemed, in fact, as though it had been able to create its own vacuum.

Simmer did not move for a long time. He stayed animal-still as his eyes traced what he knew would be the route for the interstate. He saw it coming up through the opening of the valley in the very far distance, sleeking its way across the flatland nearer the town, and then, with a great rush, hurling itself above the town and off to the west away from the mountain.

Simmer was waiting for some confirmation, some sign that would tell him it was all right to move. When he did, he was like a statue moving off its pedestal. He seemed to need a few seconds to find out that he was once again human. He walked slowly to his small office in front of the building, and, inside, he stood for a moment and looked around. Finally he went to the gun rack on the side wall and took down his deer rifle. Next, moving to the counter that held his cash register, he reached inside and took out a box of cartridges. He emptied the box on the counter top and then carefully loaded the rifle. The remaining shells he put into his pants pockets. Then he turned, took a sign from under the rack, and went to the door. He hung the sign on the inside of the door, flipped the lock, and went out toward the road. As he passed the pumps he turned and looked back at the sign: HUNTING.

In a few seconds Simmer crossed the road, the rifle slung easily through the crook of his elbow, his hands deep in his pockets; then he was gone into the woods. He disappeared by degrees among the trees and shrubs. One moment he was wholly visible; the next, he seemed to blend in and around some trees; then he would disappear completely for another few seconds, only to become once again completely visible. But with each step he took it was as if he were pulling blankets of foliage about him, one covering his legs, another his shoulders, until finally he was out of sight.

Simmer had not gone more than a hundred yards when he began to feel a transformation come over him. His first few steps into the woods had left him almost breathless. His mouth hung open, sucking in great gulps of air with nearly every step he took. His heart was some kind of fierce piston that was running with a great force all its own. But as he slowly moved away from the road, his breathing and heart rate eased off to that of a well-trained athlete, and when he could no longer see the road or his garage, his blood took on a kind of heat he had never felt before.

Blending easily into the woods, he covered the first mile in a relaxed and upright position. But the instant he heard the first sound of the heavy machinery from the construction site he crouched instinctively. Instantly the rifle was in both his hands, and he moved forward in the way he imagined soldiers had in World War I. He used the weapon to move the branches out of the way, and several times, when he thought he was a good deal closer to the site than he was, he flopped down on his belly and snapped the rifle to his shoulder. When no enemy showed himself, he sprang up and again moved off toward the construction sounds.

The last quarter-mile to the site was almost entirely up a long hill, and just before Simmer got to the top he paused and sat on the ground. For a long time he sat there, looking crumpled and used up, like a man who has run out of sitting strength and at any instant will fall over. He stared down to the ground, the rifle in his lap, his legs crossed, and gently rubbed his hand through the soft pine needles that were all around him. Every now and again as he rested he brought a handful of the needles to his face and smelled them. Then he put several in his mouth, chewed them slowly until they were small soft bits, and then swallowed them. He repeated the action several times, and then, for a kind of perverse dessert, he scraped up some dirt with his forefinger and brought it to his mouth. He tasted it tentatively with his tongue, rolled the soft brown earth between his finger and thumb, and then rubbed what was left over his lips.

He rose and went to the top of the hill, where the whole expanse of the highway was completely visible. Below him and several hundred yards into the distance the small bulldozers, giant dump trucks, bucket loaders and other machinery moved over the whole area. They seemed to Simmer to be playing with the land, moving it as and when they wished. Groups of men stood in twos and threes, talking and occasionally pointing toward an area still to be cleared.

Simmer watched from behind two small rocks for a long time, and he did not set the rifle on the rocks until he saw Sorenson's car come up over the rise at the other end of the valley and move very slowly along the brown unfinished grade of the road. It was then that his eyes seemed for an instant to become telescopic, and he was sure that for one fleeting second he was able to see Sorenson's face through the windshield. But then his eyes began to blur, and it was very difficult for him even to keep the station wagon in focus.

He did not really bring the gun to his shoulder so much as he bent slightly down to it. As if he were afraid his eyes would fail him completely, he began to shoot immediately. He pulled off three rounds very quickly, and when he raised his cheek from the butt, he expected to see Sorenson's car somehow shattered and exploded, the construction workers everywhere scattering for cover. He expected a war to be on.

What he saw was that nothing had happened. A couple of the workers were looking up from their groups in the way a hunter will pause for a moment on hearing the distant shot of another hunter. The car moved on slowly, and the machinery ground its heavy noises harder into the land.

Simmer was furious. He shot again and again, but the more he fired, the more he was ignored. The noise from the bulldozers and other machinery down in the little valley covered each report of the rifle, and after a few more minutes none of the workers even bothered to look up when Simmer fired. When his rifle was empty, Simmer stayed where he was for a long time. Then slowly he seemed to crumple down along the barrel of the gun, looking a little as if he were crying softly. Then for a few moments he was still, and when he raised his head his whole face looked as if he had died just a few seconds before. His eyes were dry and fixed in their sockets, and the little smudges of dirt around his lips looked now as if they belonged there. "See me," he said softly, and then in an instant he was standing up, his body more fully erect and taller than it had ever been, and he began to shout, "See me, see me!"

But his voice was a hundred times less effective than the rifle had been, and he knew that no one in the little valley heard him. He paused for a moment and looked around as though suddenly his whole life depended on someone's taking notice of him. Quickly he unbuttoned his shirt and stripped it from his body. As he snapped it back and over his shoulders, he revealed a trunk so massive and full of muscle that it could have at any moment simply exploded. The only thing that appeared old in any way was the skin that covered him. It seemed in places to be an old wrapping for the body of a prizefighter, and when he stood motionless for just a moment the skin dominated and controlled all that was beneath it. But when Simmer began to wave the shirt over his head, the muscles, tendons and ligaments rippled and snapped in what seemed a very private and perfectly understood relationship.

Almost immediately he saw that one of the bulldozer operators had noticed him, but Simmer was angered that the man lifted his hand, raised his hard hat a little, and gave a return wave; then, before he could see Simmer bring the rifle to his shoulder, he was once again concentrating on the gears on his machine. Simmer fired at him, but all he saw was a little puff of dirt about twenty-five yards to the right of the machine. He fired again, and the same little explosion of earth repeated itself. "See me," he said again as he sighted once more along the barrel, but then his body seemed hit by a hot stiff gust of wind and he appeared to sag all over. It was as if fatigue had suddenly become some kind of person that was assuming control of his body. The muscles of his torso appeared to go flaccid all at once, and the large triangular muscles that ran from his armpits deep into his back shook together, and then in the next instant they were no longer able to support the rifle. He half-fell, half-staggered over the two rocks in front of him, then corkscrewed downward and sat bewildered, looking back into the woods.

He sat there for a very long time with his legs straight out, his hands folded serenely in his lap, for all the world like someone who has just finished a fine picnic lunch.

His mind floated and moved freely over his past as he thought briefly of the hundreds of days he had hunted deer on the mountain with Culver and how throughout the years it had become their secret that Simmer was nearly blind in his right eye.

Calvin Runners's wife committed suicide in a way that clearly said she wanted to give herself as much pain as she could before she died.

Beginning with the night back in March when Sorenson had first come to town meeting, Estelle Runners had gone straight downhill. On the way back to their house she had become hysterical in the street. She cried openly and loud, and every few steps she flung her arms about as though to attack some unseen animal. Although Calvin Runners had tried to console her, to stay up with her at night through her ever-deepening depression, he was of very little help. All his attempts to comfort her were simple statements like, "We can stand the move," and, "No use crying over spilt milk." But Sorenson's announcement that the town was to be razed seemed to deliver an instantly fatal blow. It was as though throughout the spring and summer she were really already dead and only needed that time to let her body catch up to her mind.

She made two attempts on her life. The first one was genuinely stupid, and because it was so silly, people in the town dismissed it as a bid for attention and sympathy. She tried to hang herself in the barn, and no doubt she would have succeeded had it not been that the rope she used was a couple of feet too long to get the job done properly. She jumped out of the loft with the rope around her neck and found herself sitting on the floor of the barn between two piles of fresh horse dung. The rope, fully outstretched, had burned her neck severely. She also broke an ankle, which sent her to the hospital in Newfield. Calvin Runners was very upset, and when he told the doctors in Newfield about her attempted suicide, they were very much concerned. But that concern was diminished by Estelle Runners's glowing and thoroughly charming personality during the week she had to stay in the hospital. For the first time since town meeting she was happy, and everyone in the hospital was delighted to have her around. Her performance was magnificent because it was real.

What the doctors could not have known was that her happiness came from her having made the decision to kill herself. As far as Estelle Runners was concerned her problems and her life were over. It was just a matter of when.

She finally succeeded the afternoon of the first of August. A short while after he got back from Simmer's Garage, Calvin Runners found his wife dying in their bedroom. With a piece of brand-new clothesline she had hanged herself from the doorknob of the bedroom door. This time she had measured the rope carefully. From her position, ugly and grotesque, she seemed to be suspended in the act of seating herself on an invisible chaise longue. One leg was straight out before her, the other curled around and useless beneath her. When Calvin Runners found her she was still alive, but by the time he got the rope off and called an ambulance she was dead.

Five

It seemed that Sorenson's final offers reacted chemically with Estelle Runners's death, and the effect was to finally defeat a good number of the sternest holdouts in the town. During the two weeks following her funeral, a lot of those still left in the town accepted Sorenson's offer and prepared to move out. The way they went about it was much more significant than the fact that they were finally beaten. They gave up individually, without really saying anything to anyone about it, and even when they ran into one another at the post office they did not speak. Those who sold out, like Hal Bitterley, suddenly seemed already removed from the town. Nothing really mattered to them, not even the money. They became exiles in their own town, and people like Millie and Moose behaved like bullying children when they dealt with them. As Moose said to Bitterley one morning in the post office, "You know, for guts you got rabbit droppings."

Bitterley's whole frame became taut and he stood erect as he looked at Moose and said politely, "I do not have to defend myself to you."

"You got to put accounts right with yourself," Moose told him.

"In all of this," Bitterley said directly, "what I cannot

understand is the stubbornness of you and Mrs. Barnhope and Selectman Simmer."

"Well, I'd say that's our business."

"Unquestionably true," Bitterley said, going to the
door. He paused for a moment and then turned to
Moose. "How long do you intend to stay?" he asked.

"Forever," Moose said.

"A lot of us will be waiting to see how long that is."

Millie, though, was more civil to Bitterley. "But where
will you go?" she asked him on the afternoon when he
signed the final papers with Sorenson.

"Newfield," he said. "We're buying a house in the new
subdivision." Then he added, "It's all-electric." He said
it as if he did not know what it meant. "Most of the
people have gone to Newfield," he added. "Some I've
talked to say they like it better now that they're settled.
They got all the utilities underground." Then, without
either of them saying another word, Bitterley turned and
left the store.

It went that way with several of the others, too. One
day they collected their mail at the post office, and the
following day Moose taped a white X over the mouth of
the box. By Labor Day those still left in Oldenfield num-
bered seventeen, and some of those had promised Sorenson to leave at appointed times.

On Tuesday after Labor Day the mail truck from Concord did not come, and when Moose telephoned to ask
about the delay he was told that the Oldenfield post
office had been reclassified and that mail would now
come only three times a week. "Just like that?" Moose
thrust into the phone, and the supervisor answered
Moose with, "Just like that."

"I'm going to appeal the ruling," Moose said.

"To who?" the supervisor answered. "What you got
left up there—ten, twelve at the most?"

"I got seventeen full-time boxes."

"Well, just real good," Moose was told. "You're lucky as hell to still be on the route."

And the people from the telephone company began to come to the town more regularly to remove the phones from the houses and to take down the lines that were no longer in use. The electric company followed directly on their heels, and throughout the town most of the utility poles stood naked and useless, the wires from them wrapped securely on giant spools that sat everywhere about the town like silly garden tables. In a way it was as if all the clocks in the town had stopped too. Time seemed lifted out of its understandable pattern of numbers, elevated to some chilling abstraction that could be measured only by the speed with which the leaves were dying. One morning in the town it was late summer, the next morning true fall. The leaves changed color as if individually they had been shot and then all together had begun to bleed. The summer hurried itself out, winding down quickly into what were now vast empty spaces between the houses, and for many days an ever-thinning air hurried about the town and among those who were left. The town seemed sterilized, almost as if it had been thoroughly prepared for its death and then had simply been able to stop the process through its own will power.

Sorenson disappeared from the town soon after Labor Day. In fact, he was gone within hours after the surveyors and rodmen had finished laying out the stakes through the town. The path of the interstate was as nearly dead center as it could be, and when the people traced the route the road would take, they found that the only part of the town that would remain untouched was the cemetery. In some cases the stakes were nearly twenty feet high, depending on the roll of some of the back yards and low pastures, and the way they towered over some of the one-story houses declared that they respected nothing but the concrete and iron that would follow as straight as a line could be drawn.

Even though Sorenson was not in the town, his presence was everywhere felt through the sounds from the highway as it daily drew nearer. In a strange way his not being there seemed to kill the town faster, and several of those still left just disappeared overnight and were not heard of again. Nor, after a couple of days, was there talk about them. Only one thing was clear to those still committed to staying in the town: the road was racing the weather. In the second week in September, even before the leaves had begun to dry out completely and stiffen on the trees, the people talked of snow. "What we're needing this year," Moose said one morning in the post office, "is like back then in the forties."

Culver and Simmer nodded their understanding, but Millie was baffled. "And what happened then?" she asked.

"The Columbus Day storm," Moose said, so proudly it appeared for an instant he had caused it all by himself. "Nineteen inches overnight," he added.

"Earliest snow's ever been to stay," Simmer said. He was looking out the window the way one looks at a painting.

"In all the years I been here," Millie said, "it hasn't snowed but once before Thanksgiving. And three times before Christmas."

"Weather all over the world's getting warmer," Moose said.

"Absolutely," Culver said.

"Snow before the middle of November," Simmer put in, "—chances are maybe fifty-fifty."

"If that," Moose said.

But for all their hoping, even keeping what might well be called a permanent vigil, the weather did not change through almost all of September. The days were warm, some of them almost uncomfortably so; the wind was only a wafting trivial breeze that moved about the town in warm hunks, and night after night a giant moon hung in the sky like a great orange and yellow toy. Just the year before, everyone in the town would have agreed that it was one of the most beautiful Indian summers in many decades. The daytime sky was a crystalline kind of blue that seemed to have behind it layers of barely visible gold. It was a vast permanent ball of blue and blue, a great container that seemed to have captured puffs of painted clouds that looked like artillery flak. The only change that slid into the sky did so in a secret, quiet way. All along the rim of the horizon little blotches and patches of clouds seemed to be gathering quietly of their own accord. In places they themselves looked a little like small villages in silhouette.

Sorenson came back the first week in October, driving the station wagon through the town slowly, as if he were on vacation and enjoying a drive through the changing foliage. The trees in the town looked no more than ten minutes past peak color, and they would have been even more beautiful had they not been so thinned out. The leaves were slow to fall; and it seemed that somehow those from the innermost branches had fallen first, leaving the trees with a shell-like covering of leaves bursting with final color. All the trees seemed to be waiting for one good rainstorm, when they would overnight be stripped completely, their leaves all around the ground in shiny leather patches.

Sorenson went first to Simmer's Garage, and when he could not get Simmer to come out to the pumps he went to the front door and looked in through the glass. He saw Simmer sitting inside in an old straight-backed chair staring out at the woods through a side window. When Sorenson banged on the glass, Simmer turned and waved him away at once.

As if a little frightened, Sorenson hurried to his car and drove off quickly. As he rounded the slight turn near the far end of town, for just an instant he saw the whole town laid out before him. It seemed to him then that he was on some huge vacant lot and that the houses that lined the main street were really only assembled debris, so much garbage and trash that had to be removed. Halfway up the street Millie's store seemed for a second to huddle itself down as though to form a fierce barrier. Sorenson wanted to accelerate and drive the station wagon right through the store, simply pull it down around its foundation as swiftly as he could. He slowed the car a little, and as he passed the first set of surveyor stakes he felt a real excitement roll through him, and in a flash he wanted to turn the station wagon and follow the sleek thin line where the highway would finally go.

When he got to the post office he found Moose sitting in his small office in the back. Like Simmer, Moose seemed to be in some kind of meditation, lost somewhere in his past life. As Sorenson leaned into the little window Moose said, "There's nothing for you."

"Enjoying your reclassification?"

"You get them to do that?" Moose asked. His head snapped up as though he'd heard a gunshot.

"I brought certain figures to the attention of the postal authorities," Sorenson said.

"They ain't cut my pay," Moose told him.

"All things in good time."

"What the hell do you want here?"

"I'm putting up notices," Sorenson told him.

"Put up what you like."

"They go everywhere."

"All right," Moose said, "I'll bite."

"Condemnation notices," Sorenson answered.

Moose bolted from his chair and stood facing Sorenson. "What the hell kind of right you think you got?"

"Hazards all through the town," Sorenson said.
"When we start through, no citizen can be within the
limits of the town."

"Right on schedule."

"I will begin to raze this town on November fourteenth," Sorenson said. Then he added: "At seven o'-
clock sharp."

"We'll still beat you," Moose said from somewhere
deep inside him. But he was not looking at Sorenson,
and from the way he spoke it was clear that he wasn't
even talking to him.

"Most especially I'm going to enjoy knocking down
this silly building you've called a post office."

"You'd drive the 'dozer yourself," Moose said.

"No, not on this one. But if it were a larger building
I'd personally set the charges where they'd go."

"Answer me just one question," Moose said. "Why do
you act like some crazed crazy dog?"

"Don't you say that about me," Sorenson said quietly.

Sorenson suddenly looked as if he were on the edge
of his own sanity. There was an instant when Moose felt
a slight wave of concern roll through him, a brief second
when he thought that probably he should leave the matter there. But then he went at Sorenson's throat. "You
know what I think?" he said. "I think you got problems
above your collar."

Sorenson's head moved slightly to the side as though
he were having trouble hearing Moose. Then his eyes
bulged a little as Moose said, "The first condemned sign
you put up ought to go right to the side of your head."
But Sorenson had suddenly tuned him out. He turned
like a sad little puppet and moved toward the door.
Moose came to the window, and as Sorenson opened the
door he said, "You can put your goddamn signs anywhere you want. Put them all over the buildings like

shingles. I don't give a flying goddamn." As he stood watching through the front window, he saw Sorenson go to the back of the station wagon and take out a sign that looked to Moose to be at least three feet square. He tacked it onto the front of the building just to the right of the door, and then, without looking at the sign, without even glancing up at the building, he went to his car and drove away.

By noon there were nearly thirty signs hanging on the trees and buildings along the main street.

As they did a few nights each week, almost in a way that they themselves did not understand, they met at Millie's store that evening. Nothing was ever prearranged about it; there was simply something unseen that nudged them individually in the direction of the store. That night Simmer was first, and he came through the front door of the store as though he were going into his own living room. He glanced at Millie in a quick little flash, then looked over the empty shelves and the stark beverage cases in the back. He stood for a few minutes next to the Franklin stove, apparently listening to the low mumbling fire. Then without saying anything to Millie he sat on a small barrel that had once held nails. Looking like a giant sitting on something no bigger than a mushroom, slowly he rocked the small barrel back and forth under him. "You seen them signs," he said to the floor. Millie did not answer him. "Like we had the whooping cough."

Millie sat in the tattered lawn chair, the broken strips of the seat dangling down under her. Her elbow rested on the thin metal arm of the chair, and her hand held her head as if it were an oversized grapefruit. She stared at the door, her head over to one side as though she wished to see things at some crazy angle. "I'm done," she said. "All in and all done." She sounded like a sad auctioneer closing off final bidding.

Simmer looked at her for a long time, then dropped his head as though to agree in silence.

Culver and Moose came in together, each carrying a loose white bundle. Millie's whole frame snapped rigid as she raised a hand and pointed at the bundles as though her action would take the place of speech.

"The signs," Culver said with great pride. He put his stack on the long empty counter in front of Millie. "Moose ripped down every single one of them."

Moose's face glowed like a proud child's as he put his stack on top of Culver's and then picked several of the signs from the top of it. He shuffled them together, then turned and with great care began to feed them into the open mouth of the Franklin stove. Finally, after a few moments, Millie said, "I think we're done."

"Done what?" Moose shot at her from the stove.

"Finished," she said. There was a general collapsing of her trunk, as though the breath she had used to make the statement had been her last. A look of great distance grabbed at her head and face.

Culver looked quickly at Moose, a little afraid that he would be the next to quit, but Moose was looking past him at Millie. "Just what the hell you talking about?" Moose said. "Where you think you come by the right to pack up?"

"Way inside here," she said. She tapped the middle of her chest with a forefinger.

"My goddamn heart bleeds," Moose said.

"Stop it," Millie said quietly.

"No more, no more," Simmer said from his little stool.

Millie came up out of her chair and stood leaning on the counter. "All right, Superman," she said to Moose. "You go out there and pick up those 'dozers and backhoes and you cart them away."

Then there was an ugly silence in the store, but a silence with a direction. It was as though all their energies suddenly focused on Moose's squat form in front of the stove. Methodically he tore the signs, put them in the stove, and then held his position as the fire shot up. He stayed that way for a long time, the only change being the color of his face. Each time the fire ballooned it seemed as if it transferred some of its energy directly to him, and when he finally stood up his face glowed as if he had caught the fire with his hands and buried his face in it. He looked at Millie, Culver and Simmer, and then he said, "Let's steal the goddamn town. When that son of a bitch ain't looking, let's us take our houses and buildings and clear them out of here, take them somewheres he ain't."

"You grab one end, I'll take the other," Simmer said. A thin stupid smile crossed his face as his gaze slid down Moose's body and crawled back to the floor at his own feet. Millie and Culver, though, stood as though they expected Moose to go on, and then each turned to the other as though for an answer. "We sell out," Moose quickly went on, "and then we use the money to move the town." He paused to consider the enormity of what he had just said. "Or as much of it as we can."

"You'll need a pretty big van," Simmer said, shaking his head and laughing a little in a private way.

"Shut up, Carl," Culver said without taking his eyes from Moose.

"It's nonsense," Millie said. It was clear that she would not consider it.

"I don't know," Culver said. His eyes blinked in quick little bursts, as though a great sequence of rapid-fire calculations were taking place just behind them. "I don't know."

"Somebody tell me why the hell not," Moose said. His voice was weak now, quivering and almost afraid, and it was very doubtful whether his mind could really comprehend the meaning of what he had just said. If he could have, he would have passed his first remark on to someone else; he wanted no responsibility for it.

In the next few moments Culver seemed to take charge of the future. It was almost as though the others gave up some of their energy to Culver, who appeared to take on an authority he had never before had. It was as though his whole life in the town had suddenly been given a meaning he could see and feel. His body seemed in the next few moments to slim itself, to grow quickly stronger and rigid, each cell bright and ready. In those few moments time raced ahead for Culver, as though seasons became seconds that moved by in quick flashes, and in his mind there was an enormous, vast opening out of which rose a vision that instantly made his blood sing. He saw Oldenfield crushed and flattened by Sorenson's bulldozers, the interstate sleek and serene in its own concrete harmony, but out of it all he saw the town rising up again out of fresh woods in a greener place and another more perfect time.

"It could be done," he said to the others, but when he looked closely at each of them he saw that only Moose registered the slightest belief, and even he dropped his eyes to the floor when Culver started to go on. Then Culver stopped himself and looked closely at Millie. She seemed removed to some far-off place, as though she were still in Connecticut and coming to Oldenfield had never really happened to her.

But Simmer was worse. He was shoved so far back into the past that for a moment Culver thought it would now be impossible ever to reach him again. His head was tilted slightly to one side, the silly grin fixed on it as though by some perverse artist.

Culver turned to Moose and said quietly, "Do you know what I'm saying?"

Moose looked up slowly, his eyes moving in little grinding inches all the way up Culver's body, and when their gazes locked for a second Moose nodded once. "But it's crazy," he said softly.

"It is that," Culver answered. The first surge of power

that had risen in him now seemed to even out, and he stood like a great idling motor.

"There isn't any way," Millie said, so quietly that it appeared she was talking to some invisible person next to her. Culver saw Simmer shake his head in silent agreement.

"Ask a question," Culver said, "any question, about it." His confidence was almost arrogance, and he saw that in Millie's bewilderment her only reaction was anger.

"I'm telling you," she threw at him.

"Where?" Moose said. "You tell us where we move it to."

In Millie's face Culver saw that the question had registered as if she had asked it herself, and she stood looking at him with a fierce urgency. "My land," he said, "the acreage that runs along the lake and up toward the mountain. There's any number of flat places."

"Your land," Simmer said. "I suppose you'll want to be Selectman."

"Goddamn it, man," Culver shouted, "if you want, I'll deed it all right now. I'll get the papers and sign them over this goddamn minute."

Millie raised her hand in front of her to stop Culver and Simmer, and after a long moment she said, "Maybe, just maybe."

In another few moments huge plans began to unfold in their minds, and each person talked in little spurts without really addressing the others. Every now and again one of them asked Culver a serious and direct question, and with each answer he gave, the little group seemed to grow more excited and more deliberate. The only one who dragged behind in the excitement was Simmer, and after about fifteen minutes he suddenly said to the others, "What I want to know is why we're doing this."

"To beat that bastard Sorenson into the ground,"
Moose said proudly.

"No," Culver said quickly. "It's to keep the town as
best we can the way it is."

"You can't take the whole thing," Simmer said. His
hands made a round sweeping gesture in front of him.

"We take the store," Culver said. He pointed a finger
toward the floor and jabbed at it several times. "The post
office, Carl's place," he went on.

"Your house, too," Moose put in.

"And if there's a way under God's sun," Culver said,
"we take town hall."

Simmer's head tilted back as if he were following a
flock of geese as he said, "You know what it weighs, how
high it is?"

"We take it if we can," Culver repeated.

"There ain't a crane this side of Boston that'll handle
it," Simmer said.

"If that's how it is," Culver answered, "then we go to
the other side of Boston."

"What the hell is all of this going to cost?" Moose
suddenly put in.

"Probably pretty close to everything we get from Sorenson," Culver told him. He paused and looked at each
of the others, then went on, "If we're going to do this,
we have to say what our offers are."

Simmer's eyes shifted uneasily between Millie and
Moose.

"The money's got to be pooled," Culver went on,
"and what's left at the end of this thing goes back to each
of us on a percentage basis of what went in. My offer's
thirty thousand."

"He's jewing you," Moose said.

"Never mind that for now," Culver said. "What'd you
get?"

"The last one's thirty-nine five," he said.

"Jesus Christ," Simmer said, "that bastard says our places are equal? He won't get me to scratch that paper for him." He folded his arms across his chest and sat as if he were made of wood. Culver turned to Millie, who put her head down a little and then finally said, "Seventy-two something."

"Well now, that just says everything," Moose told the room. "Culver's place for thirty, yours for forty-something *more.*"

"Sorenson is not as stupid as one might like to think," Culver said.

Millie looked up. "He told me he was doubling it because my boy died."

"First thing in the morning," Culver said, "I'll tell Sorenson we'll sign."

"How much does it total?" Moose asked.

"A little less than two hundred thousand," Simmer put in.

"Can we move what we want for that?" Millie asked.

"We could raise the dead with that," Culver answered.

"Tell him, tell him, Culver," Moose said. He moved a little forward, and with a great warm light in his face he patted Culver on the shoulder. Then they began to laugh as waves of relief spread through them. Moose and Culver let go belly laughs that burst throughout the store; Millie's shoulders shook in spastic little vibrations; and Simmer's face, red and alive, seemed instantly to have grown young. His mouth creased in his thin warm smile of years before, and his eyes watered up in a bright kind of way.

It was Culver's face that first registered a hint of fear, and he stopped laughing almost instantly. Without saying anything, he seemed able to transmit his thoughts to the others, and in quick little moments of understanding each there knew that even though they were now of one will, that alone would not get the job done. They knew it had to snow.

True to his word, Culver was at Sorenson's door early the next morning, and Sorenson was so full of satisfaction in finally having won that he was utterly disgusting about it. "Now I have always admired bravery," he said, "but bravery put with stupidity equals insanity. You never really had a chance—you knew that from the beginning."

"It was just a matter of your being patient," Culver said.

"Precisely that," Sorenson answered.

"You bring the checks this afternoon," Culver said, "and we'll sign all the papers you got."

"Why now?" Sorenson suddenly put in. "Why all of you last ones at the same time?" It was clear that he wanted to enjoy his victory, to know every feeling of those he had beaten.

"People like us are stubborn sometimes," Culver answered, "but we're never, never stupid."

"But all of you at the same time," Sorenson said. "Oh, I knew I'd get you sooner or later, but from the beginning I was convinced I'd have to pick you off one by one."

"Do you want me to tell you you're too smart for us?" Culver said, starting for the door.

Sorenson laughed a little and said, "I wouldn't mind."

"Personally," Culver said, holding the door ajar, "I'm not quite finished with you."

The little ceremony in Millie's store that afternoon was a strange event. When Sorenson came in carrying a flat briefcase, he went directly to the counter, unzipped the case, and laid out the deeds and the bills of sale. He put each of the four checks with its papers, then handed a pen to Millie. As she signed the papers where Sorenson indicated, the others in the store crowded around and watched. No one spoke a word. It was as though Sorenson were a true and final enemy of the others, each sufficiently afraid of the other to guard his own ground before thinking of attack. One by one they signed after Millie, and as Sorenson gathered up the papers, they examined their checks with great suspicion. Then as Sorenson secured his briefcase he looked around at those standing there as though he wanted to say something but needed someone to tell him to speak, to say that it would be best to get off his chest whatever it was he wanted to.

But he got no help from anyone, and when they were satisfied that the checks were good and real, their gazes lifted, fixing with a certain final horror on Sorenson. They all seemed to be speaking to him with their eyes. Immediately clear was the hate that Sorenson had engendered in all of them, as though back at the town meeting in March he had given them all a transfusion of slow-acting hate and only now was it finally boiling up in them. But their hate was beyond that for another person. The hate seemed to be for the very processes of life itself.

They stood like five statues, growing more silent with every second that slid by.

Finally, it was Sorenson who moved. As though controlled by strings, he turned away from the group and walked slowly to the door. As he stopped for a moment with his back to the others, the fading afternoon twilight captured him completely. He looked a little as if he would just slide through the closed door and be sucked up and away into the falling afternoon. For a few more seconds Sorenson stood hunched, growing smaller the longer he stood there. Then without a sound he was out the door and gone immediately into the dusk.

The next morning Culver was at Simmer's Garage a little before six. He pulled his truck close to the front window and hit the horn. When Simmer came out of the back, Culver waved to him, and as Simmer opened the door with an angry, bewildered expression, Culver held up a long roll of paper. "Come on, now," he shouted at Simmer. "There're things to do."

Simmer looked up at the sky as though to give it a careful check as he said, "What now?"

"Get your truck, your saw, and follow me."

"Where we going?"

"We got us some land to clear."

Simmer suddenly came alive in a primitive kind of way. He looked for an instant or two as if all the strength he had used up over the years had suddenly in one flash come back into his body. His head snapped up as if he had caught some wondrous animal scent, and he seemed to be able to feel the very texture of the air around him. Quickly he went to the far side of his garage, where he scooped the chain saw from the floor, wrapping it in a small tarpaulin as if it were an infant, and in a slow, almost stumbling run he was off to his truck.

The nearest access to Culver's land was just over a mile from the post office, and when Culver got there he stopped his truck and slid the gears into four-wheel drive. Simmer followed as Culver eased off the road, through the little opening in the stone boundary fence, and started across the fields toward the first heavy stand of pines.

When Culver could no longer maneuver his truck, he stopped it, turned off the ignition and got out. He stood for a moment oblivious of Simmer, and then, without looking at him or even knowing whether he was beside him, Culver raised his hand in a precise direction and said, "Over there, through the second stand and a little beyond. Things open up and the slope is near to what we're after." Still without taking any notice of Simmer, Culver went around to the passenger side of the truck, and from behind the seat in the cab he took out his chain saw. Then almost as though it were an afterthought he snatched the long rolled-up paper from the seat. He put the chain saw down into the soft brown grass, saying, "Come here." As Simmer approached, Culver unrolled the paper and, arms outstretched, held it securely on the hood of the truck. He let Simmer look at it for several moments before he said, "You think it's right enough?"

"It is," Simmer answered. He was looking at a drawing of the two main streets of Oldenfield. Sketched lightly, but in perfect proportion, were the dimensions of all the house lots as they still existed in the town. "Is there much to clear?" Simmer asked.

"Sixty, maybe seventy trees," Culver answered. He ran his hand down the right side of the plans. "Mostly all along this side," he said.

"Let's see it."

Moving off from the trucks with their chain saws slung down by their knees, the two men looked as though they were simply off to cut firewood. As they came out of the stand of pines, their whole frames shook from the great roar that came tumbling over the mountain in the distance and moved through the valley like a giant bulldozer. Culver and Simmer looked at each other, and in both their faces was absolute fear. It seemed to them that with the signing of the papers Sorenson had commanded the highway to take a huge leap forward, and from the nearness of the explosion neither of them doubted that it would be only a matter of days before the first great bulldozer chugged right up the main street of the town.

They waited a few moments while the sound of the explosion pealed away among the distant woods and died. Culver turned to Simmer and once again held the map for him. "From here," he said with a sweep of his arm, "do you see where it's to go?"

Simmer's gaze swept the gentle rolling land in front of him, and he appeared for a moment to see the whole town in front of him. He turned slightly and looked back over his shoulder as if he might see the road to his gas station already in place. "Where you want me to start?" Simmer asked.

Culver tapped the top of the map just beyond the rectangular drawing of town hall, and Simmer nodded. "First we string a line all along the right side," Culver said, "and then we'll clear it all back no less than forty feet. That'll give the 'dozer all the room she needs." Simmer nodded again, and this time he took the line from Culver and started off through the raspberry bushes and the small thin trees. Culver watched him for nearly a hundred yards before Simmer's figure was lost completely among the shrubs.

At a hundred and fifty yards Culver shouted for Simmer to stop, and he did so almost before the sound of Culver's voice had a chance to reach him. Culver secured the line under a rock, and then in a smooth, comfortable motion he slipped his hatchet from his belt. Almost as if he were reaching out to pat the small sapling near him, he cut it on a perfect angle at its base. The tree stood for a second next to its stump, and as it began to fall Culver trimmed it into a stake with short easy passes of the hatchet. In two minutes Culver had the line tied to the stake as though it had always been there.

Within a few minutes both the chain saws came alive in the woods, and for hours after that it was as if they were two people talking back and forth over a huge distance. Almost in perfect rhythm and unison, when one slowed and whined down, the other revved ever higher in a metallic counterpoint. Sometimes their sounds layered over each other, and instead of the roar doubling in its effect, it seemed to peak in a geometric growl. The trees fell along the back side of where the houses would go almost as though they knew they were doomed. They went over one by one in their own liquid ways, their branches reaching out to those on trees still standing. The sounds they made were like great rustling gusts of breath, but when they hit the ground they bounced lightly and seemed content finally to be down.

Culver and Simmer worked along a line toward each other, and by noon they stood side by side, each looking at what the other had done. "You're a little wobbly up by that spruce," Culver said.

"You go right to hell," Simmer told him.

They stood for a few more minutes with the sawdust in sweaty streaks across their faces and foreheads, and every now and again one of them brushed a fresh chip of wood from his jacket. "I got a bucket loader coming at one," Culver said, "and then all we got to do is pile it up and set a match to it."

Sorenson came to the post office early that morning, looking as if he had spent the night on the rack. His face was a sloppy mess of random lines that in the last eighteen hours had been cut noticeably deeper. His hair had clearly been not combed but sorted out by hand and arranged in a random way on his head. He carried with him the deeds signed the night before at Millie's store. "These are to go *registered*," he told Moose as he slid the bulky little package across the worn counter.

Moose weighed it, put the small book of registered materials in front of Sorenson, and then started to fill out the little yellow slip. He told him the price and put the stamps on it, and then as he ran the killer bars over the stamps he looked at Sorenson and said, "You jackass."

"You'll never give up, will you?" Sorenson said. His face had eased into a tired, almost relaxed expression.

"We ain't played none of our aces yet," Moose said.

Sorenson's eyes snapped up quickly and searched Moose's face, seeing in it something fiercely genuine, and for a moment he wanted to reach out and take back the package with the deeds.

But Moose beat him to it. He slid the package off the counter and, without even looking, tossed it squarely into the one large gray mailbag still standing in the rack alongside the wall to his right. "Done," he said, "within the safe hands of the United States government."

"What are your aces?"

"Isn't that just for me to know," Moose said.

"You try anything illegal," Sorenson said, "and I'll have you locked up so fast you won't know what hit you." He held up his receipt.

"It's all perfectly legal," Moose said.

"You'd better say," Sorenson told him. "You cause me any trouble . . ."

"We'll just be taking what's ours," Moose told him.

"And what's that?"

"The houses, you simpleton," Moose said. "We're going to take what's ours and put them where you can't ever do nothing to us."

In the moment of release Moose looked immediately done in and defeated. It was as though Sorenson had instantly gone deaf, and when Moose could get no reaction from him he yelled, "You simpleton." But even after a few more seconds Sorenson looked as if he still did not hear Moose.

Then, as though some long and fantastic joke had finally spread through him, he began to laugh. It was a silly little laugh, almost startling in its absurd contrast to the size of the person laughing. It was as if only Sorenson's head were laughing, as though his body for a long time had gone to solid rock. Finally after a few minutes he said, "My God, you people," and he turned and went out of the post office. As he got into his station wagon, another wave of laughter slammed into him and shook his little head.

Later that afternoon, as Sorenson was shouting instructions to one of the teams of surveyors, he suddenly looked into the far distance and saw a thin column of rising smoke. He turned away from the man in front of him, and suddenly he felt totally bewildered. His gaze quickly scanned the soft line of hills all around, and when he saw that there was only one small fire he looked relieved. Then suddenly things began to click in his head, and what Moose had told him in the post office suddenly became intuitively true. He pushed past the men in front of him and headed for his station wagon. Just before he started the car he noticed that the column of smoke had grown thicker and more menacing. He drove toward it as though he had been over the route many times, and as the car moved along through the town and then out Route 10 and by the lake, he lost control of himself utterly and completely.

There had always been about him a feeling that he had been wound too tight, that at almost any moment he would explode in a sad and meaningless way. He seemed to have the capacity to blow himself up, to take all his real energy and in one instant dissolve it into the wind. This was happening to him in the car in quick little segments. In small bursts from some green and turgid tumor in his spirit a kind of poison oozed all through him, and when he came parallel to Culver's land and saw the fire leaping up from the cleared site, he was finally in another world. He parked the car near the opening in the boundary fence and sat for a long time, looking out at the fields and the fire. Then, as though the final anger of his life had just hit him, he was out of the car and walking toward the fire.

He found Culver and Simmer on the far edge of the site. Culver was standing with his arms folded across his chest, and Simmer, looking tired and worn out from the morning's work, was squatting precariously on the large metal handle of his chain saw. As he watched the fire he rocked back and forth a little.

It was Culver who saw Sorenson first, and with a little nod he drew Simmer's attention. The men faced each other at a distance of twenty or so yards, and for a long moment they locked in a fierce stare-down. The only thing that gave life to the scene was the rising and falling of the flames from the huge fire that partially separated them.

Finally Culver raised his hand with what appeared to be tremendous authority. The hand unraveled from the arm, and one powerful finger held Sorenson in its sight. "You may not be on this land," Culver said in a voice that seemed to make Sorenson's figure grow smaller. "You must put yourself off it now."

Sorenson's face cracked into a weird and strange smile. "I'm not going to let you do this," he said, his muffled voice blending with the soft roar from the fire.

"His wits are mixed," Simmer said. He rose slowly and turned to face Sorenson. He stood straddling his chain saw, his hands on his hips, and watched Sorenson begin to move toward them.

Sorenson came straight on through a little patch of burning grass, taking no notice as his feet scuffed up little bursts of gray smoke.

"You'd better hold it there," Culver said. "You've no claim to where you stand."

"This is Culver's land," Simmer confirmed.

"You're not going to do this to me," Sorenson said. Suddenly he looked around in true panic, as though death had assumed the form of everything around him and now waited to claim him, too. When he saw Culver's chain saw lying some ten to twelve feet away, he was on it so fast that what he was doing hardly had time to register with Culver. Sorenson snatched it from the ground and brought it to his chest with a kind of frantic affection. His eyes searched it quickly, and then slowly he looked up at Culver and Simmer, who decided that for all practical purposes he was finally crazy. His face was broken up into small bits and fractions of feelings that everywhere showed themselves in stark and horrible contrasts. Part of his mouth was locked in a fantastic smile, the other part flat and rigid as though it could never again show any feeling. His eyes glared with some private and unspeakable vision, and above them his forehead ran down in heavy thick lines toward his right eyebrow. "Now," he shouted, "you will not, do you hear me? You will *not!*"

Culver and Simmer glanced at each other, and then Culver took two steps toward Sorenson. That was the trigger. Sorenson dropped the chain saw, put his foot through the metal handle, and gave one vicious yank to the starting cord. The machine sprang to life at his feet like a sleeping animal suddenly commanded to kill. Culver backed up more than he advanced, holding his hand in front of him in a futile signal for Sorenson to stop all his actions immediately. From behind, Culver heard Simmer say, "He's mine," and then instantly he heard Simmer's chain saw burst with its own sound. "He's gone mad," Culver said. "Don't go near him."

"He's all I want," Simmer said, and with that he snapped the chain saw in front of him and held it for an instant in a kind of military salute. As Culver backed away, the two men began to move as though they were inscribing the inside of a large circle. They seemed, in fact, held by some invisible line, and when one of them moved forward, the other went back as though he were taking up slack. As Simmer moved, his eyes darted from Sorenson to the ground. In a few seconds he knew where every stick of wood was, where each rock broke the surface of the ground. The chain saws whirred gently in a bumping pattern, and every few seconds one of the men would press the trigger, and the saw would make a vicious ripping sound through the air.

Watching Simmer circle, Culver knew that he could not stop him from whatever he wanted to do; Simmer was a man suddenly possessed. The two men moved ever more slowly in the circle until finally they stopped and faced each other in almost the exact positions from which they had begun.

It was Sorenson who moved first. His mouth was forming tight private words, as though he were addressing a demon that had suddenly been given substance, and when he swung the chain saw at Simmer it roared past his head, and for a moment it looked as though Sorenson would himself fly into the air. Simmer countered with a quick little jab of his machine, but it did not even come close to Sorenson's body. A second thrust with the saw showed one clear thing: Simmer's strength, which had been so wondrously renewed, had flung itself from his body, and he shook a little as he stood holding the saw as though it had suddenly become an immense log. Sorenson saw Simmer's predicament even before it registered on Culver's face, and he was quick to take advantage of it. Again he began to circle Simmer, faster than Simmer could pivot. When he was a little ahead of Simmer, he thrust in again with the saw, and this time he caught the front of Simmer's jacket with the tip of the chain. Instantly a hole was sliced in the material, and for a few seconds threads floated in the still air around Simmer's head. "How is it, old man?" Sorenson threw at Simmer. "The next one'll come right out your back."

Culver started closer, but Simmer held up a hand to stop him. In the brief instant that Sorenson glanced at Culver, Simmer charged. He swung the chain saw with all his strength in a huge right-to-left arc, but Sorenson snapped himself out of the way with several feet to spare. "Pathetic," Sorenson said, looking at Simmer with a hate so violent that it seemed capable of making Simmer weaker.

"For God's sake, Carl," Culver shouted at Simmer, "put the saw down."

Holding it as best he could with the blade dangling down close to his ankle, Simmer shook his head at Culver's command. Sorenson brought the saw up across his chest and stepped toward Simmer. As he did so, Simmer tried to bring his saw into position, but his knees suddenly buckled, and he became in that instant a sad old man. He sank to his knees slowly, as though beginning a long prayerful vigil, and looked up at Sorenson. He saw in his face a stupid blankness, and the utterly vacant look infuriated him. He thrust the saw up at Sorenson with all the strength he had left, and as he pitched forward on the ground he was just able to see the blue spinning tip slice its way into Sorenson's outstretched hand. There was a long and sick moment of silence, and then Sorenson's hand quietly exploded.

He dropped his saw and it spun itself out in little chopping explosions of brown grass and dirt. Then the hand came apart all by itself. In the first seconds there was no blood at all, as if the saw when it had smashed into the hand had been able to drive the blood back up into Sorenson's arm. But then it came in spurty little rivers that shot out of the hand and fell in warm spots on the grass. Simmer shoved himself back up on his knees and stayed there, gazing at Sorenson's hand as though someone else were responsible for having ruined it. Sorenson held what was left of his hand, and then in a sickly stupid way he tried to put it in his coat pocket. He brought the hand back and moved it in a slow, futile gesture along the side of his coat. All the while the blood ran from it as though there were a pump in his arm especially for that purpose. He made little grunting throat sounds as his hand moved back and forth along the fabric of the coat.

When Culver finally came between them, he already had his jacket off, and in one hand he held a long piece of rawhide bootlace. He dropped the jacket at Sorenson's feet and in one quick motion had the rawhide around Sorenson's wrist and pulled tight. It slipped a little as it found its own place on his arm, and immediately it darkened from Sorenson's blood. The bleeding stopped as though Culver had turned off a faucet, and it was then that Sorenson looked at his hand for the first time. It looked less like a hand than like some prehistoric model for a hand. The little finger was simply gone, and the ring finger next to it was sliced open at the joint of the hand so badly that it had completely turned over and now hung from the palm only by one long thin white bone. The rest of the hand looked as if it had tried to catch an exploding grenade. The tip of the saw had gone in through the base of the little finger and then had chewed its way directly down into the palm. The heel of the hand had been literally blown away, and as Culver held it to check the bleeding, it looked as if someone had taken a huge pie slice out of it. Culver watched the hand and at the same time picked up his jacket. As he began to wrap it around Sorenson's hand, the other two fingers and thumb began to quiver and jerk on their own. They moved in spastic little motions, almost as though they were now in some futile search for any other fingers that might still be left.

Simmer got slowly to his feet and watched Culver's efforts. Then he looked into Sorenson's face. The awful burning was gone from Sorenson's eyes; the hate that had swelled his cheeks and forehead had instantly withered; and an incredible ease had blown itself all through him. With what was an almost mysterious quiet he said, "Help me, help me."

"He's got to get to Newfield," Culver said to Simmer. He turned Sorenson and began to guide him back to the stand of pines and toward his truck. "Does it hurt yet?" Culver said.

"No," Sorenson answered. His voice sounded as if he were ending a long and lovely prayer.

"It will," Culver said.

The next three days were clear and dry. In the daytime the sky gleamed a bright, washed-out blue, and at night the stars whined and whistled in their brilliance. The air, cold and wintry, amplified the sounds that came both from the highway and from Culver's land. The work pace was furious, and what drove Culver, Simmer and Moose to be at the site before first light was the fear that the cold bubble of air that sat over the whole area would freeze the ground. They knew that if that happened, no amount of heavy machinery would allow them to finish what they had begun.

The morning after Sorenson's accident Culver, Moose and Simmer were at the site a full hour before the bulldozer was due from Newfield. They stood near the remains of the fire that still gave out heat in little streams of white smoke as Culver outlined for them what they would have to do for the next three days if, he said, the weather held. "First, we make us a decent road into here," he said. "Then we bring it right up through and take it just up to where the tree line begins." He moved his hand and arm as though in one sweep it would all be done. "Then we blade off the sites, first for the store, then the post office." He looked at Simmer. "Then our places," he said to him.

"You got a backhoe for the house holes?" Moose asked.

"I got everything," Culver told him.

"Water?" Simmer said quickly. "Wells and septics?"

"I ain't walking from a stream someplace, I'll tell you that," Moose said.

"It's all here," Culver said, putting his index finger to his head.

Indeed it was all there. For the next three days they tore over the land, and Culver's directions were always clear and sharp. It was as though his mind held a perfect three-dimensional vision of the town, and to get one or another problem solved it appeared that all he had to do was open his mind and look at how he wanted the new town to be. In those three days the road was carved into the gentle rolling slope and the four building sites were cleared and leveled off. On the third day another bulldozer and two backhoes came from Newfield to dig the house holes. By dusk on that day there were the barest beginnings to the shape of the town. What had been done made the place look like a giant ragged skeleton of what still stood in Oldenfield. Because there were holes where the houses should have been, there seemed an eerie, negative quality to the place, as though somehow it had been there many years before. As the three men stood across from the house hole for Millie's store, Moose said, "It's good, Culver. It's really good."

Culver nodded. Then, as if he'd caught some special scent, he raised his head and cocked it to one side, almost as if he were tuning some spiritual inner mechanism to something no one else could see or hear. "A bit warm for last light," he said. Together the three of them slowly lifted their heads and looked at the sky. The early stars, which only an hour or so before had burned their way through the twilight haze, were in a slow way being erased from the sky by a line of fierce black clouds moving in slowly from the south and southeast.

The men turned slowly and went to their trucks. As they walked back down the new road Culver said, "Best get the plow rigs on." And then as he got into his truck he glanced once again at the line of clouds in the distant sky. "She could be all we need," he said.

It began to snow around five o'clock the next morning. There was a strange hard bite to the air, and first light came into the sky in a quiet, vague way. The snow began casually, as though it were some kind of natural after-thought, and for the first several hours it whipped through the town as though searching for something specific. The flakes were not really flakes. They felt as if all the water had been removed from them, and their effect was more that of a fine white sand that moved in little ever-changing tornadoes among the houses and along the street.

For a long time the storm stayed quiet and indecisive, but the four still left in the town seemed already pinned inside their houses. It was as though each were waiting for some sign that would tell him the storm would stay; the snow would pile up in great frozen heaps; that winter had come. About eleven o'clock the storm declared that it had a mind and purpose of its own. The wind suddenly picked up, and within a very few minutes it multiplied the amount of snow it carried.

Almost instantly things in the town began to disappear. The snow let down a great gauze blanket, and even nearby houses and trees faded from sight. By the middle of the afternoon it was clear that the storm was certainly a major one, that the snowfall would be at least a foot to fifteen inches. But even in that knowledge there was a fear that even that would not stop the highway.

"We got to have twenty inches," Culver told Millie in the store that afternoon. "And it's got to drift. We get that and not a state vehicle'll move till March."

The two of them stood, as if casually watching traffic, at her front door and looked out through the two large glass panes. "Do you think we'll get that much?" Millie asked.

"It'll be close," Culver said.

It wasn't close at all. As night began to fall, the storm grew angrier and in a way fed on its own existence. It became something fearful and supernatural in the way it attacked the town. The satisfaction that Culver and the others felt soured as the night went on. Just after midnight Culver realized that the storm was wholly out of control, that what had begun as an early winter northeaster had become a killer storm. The windows of the houses rattled mercilessly; some of the doors of the empty houses were blown in as if by some giant swift hand; and the snow itself attacked the houses as though it were suddenly furious at the fact that they existed at all. It began to find its way into cracks in the houses in such a way that it appeared to be creating them as it went.

Especially was that true at Millie's store. Sitting as it did in one of the lowest areas of the town, it took a fierce beating from the drifting. For a long time that night Millie was terrified that one whole side of her store would collapse. The wind that beat against it shot little puffs of snow through the north wall, and the cold entered the store from all sides. Nothing that she did to heat the place had any effect. In fact, the more intensely the Franklin stove burned, the swifter it seemed to draw the cold toward it. But sometime after midnight the beating against the north side of the building began to soften, and in its place was a slow and heavy creaking. Some of the ceiling plaster cracked and dropped to the floor. Millie knew why the wind seemed to have dropped off; she had known it would happen, long before the giant drift had risen up to seal over the window on that side of the house. Everything in her store was muted from the storm, and she knew that the drift was above her roof and inching its way along the shingles with every passing minute. The drift itself was like a huge white wave caught in that instant just before it breaks and roars, and the only thing preventing exactly that was the building itself.

Culver and Simmer, though, lived in areas protected by trees and little knolls, and in places it looked as though it had not snowed at all. There were sweeps of hard ground with only the barest white fuzz clinging to them, and here and there even a pile of dead frozen leaves sat totally resistant to the wind. But almost by design the post office was as exposed as it could be. The east side of it had no protection at all, and it was said that if the shot could be properly lined up, a rifle bullet from Newfield could hit it broadside. The wind and snow tumbled and smashed against it with such fury that Moose was genuinely afraid. He sat in his living room listening alternately to the gusts of wind and to the hard chugging sound of the oil burner in the basement. With the thermostat set at ninety-five, Moose sat in the living room in the heaviest coat he owned. For a long time he stared at the windows and watched the snow slip its way in and around the sashes and the sills. What made him even more afraid was that the snow, when it bunched up on the windowsills, did not melt. When several inches had piled up in long smooth lines along the sills, the snow began to slide in soft little bursts down toward the floor, and it seemed to have a mind of its own as it piled up on the wood floor and then the edge of the rug.

When the power went off at about three-thirty the sudden darkness in Culver's living room jerked him full awake. All he was able to see was the strange effect of the fireplace flaring up in each of the windows. The fire made no sound as one orange triangle of flame licked and rolled around the thinning logs.

"Oh, my Christ," Culver said as he got out of his chair. He went immediately to the telephone and began to dial even before he had the receiver off the hook. Almost instantly he realized that the phone was dead. He dropped it back into its cradle and went to warm himself by the fire. He stood there for a few moments, and then he put several fat logs on the fire. They flared up almost instantly, and when Culver was satisfied that they would maintain the warmth in the room, he went out into the hall to put on his heavy parka. As he started to go outside a great fear struck him. When he opened the front door a few little puffs of snow swirled in around his head, and then he was staring at a white wall just on the other side of the storm door. By raising himself on his toes he could just see into the black beyond it, and when he pushed against the storm door it was as though someone had nailed it shut from the outside. It did not give at all, and when Culver looked again over the top of it he saw that the drift ran out and down about twelve feet and along the whole length of the house. He went directly to the porch off the kitchen, and when he opened it he saw that it was clear. Outside, a few steps down, he saw immediately that the drift had curled around the house like the loose end of a blanket and that it stretched itself in an ever-growing wave clear to the woods. He knew then that the only way to get to the road where his truck waited was back along the L and out through the barn. He was able to open the barn doors sufficiently to get himself outside, but he didn't get much farther. He was able to half-walk, half-swim his way through the first drift, but the second was simply far too high and broad for him to make any progress at all. And he did not try very hard. He knew when he looked out that he could not make it to the road, and his effort had been made partly in anger, partly in fear. He walked back slowly through the barn and the L, and when he got to the house he realized that the temperature inside was falling very fast.

He built the fire as high as it would go, then went to one of the living room windows and looked out in the direction of the post office, the store beyond it, and Simmer's Garage still farther on. Through the large spiny tree next to the house, he could see in the sky a huge dark area that looked like an enormous thunderhead. He looked at it for a long time before he realized that the storm was breaking, that what he saw was the true black night finally lowering itself through the gray clouds.

By seven-thirty the power was back on, and it was none too soon for any of them. As the storm broke in the early morning hours, a vicious wind sprang up which seemed wholly capable of sweeping from the houses what little heat they still held. Especially was that true in Culver's house and the post office. The old solid wood in them groaned and creaked so loudly that it sounded as if aged people were everywhere snapping ligaments and tendons. Occasionally, a nail popped so forcefully from the wind and cold that it sounded like a soft gunshot. Culver was slow in digging out to his truck. It took him nearly an hour to cut a path twenty feet through the drift to the road, and when he finally got out he looked back to see that the wind had sealed over the path he had cut, that behind him it looked as though he had magically passed through the drift without ever touching it. As he got into his truck he saw Simmer heading up toward him, the plow on the front end down and angled to the side. For just an instant it looked to Culver as though Simmer were turning the snow to water. The snow furrowed up and away from the plow and fell back against itself in a tight, smooth wave. "We got to do the streets," Simmer shouted in the wind. "Ain't no state plows coming in."

"Why the hell not?" Culver yelled back.

"They said nobody lives here anymore."

They plowed the main street in tandem, and the effect was almost as if one of the state's ten-wheelers had been through. Within an hour the main street was cleared all the way down to Route 10, and both Moose and Millie were plowed out. Most of the town looked, in fact, as if it were fresh and alive and had just opened up for business. When they were finished, they parked their trucks in front of Millie's store and got out. Simmer and Culver looked at each other, and then Culver said, "We've got us a hell of a mess."

As they started into Millie's store, they were stopped abruptly by the continuous honking from Moose's car. One window was down and he was waving frantically to them. When he stopped hard on the snow the car fishtailed a little and snapped to a stop. "Get in, get in," Moose said. "Holy God, you ain't going to believe it."

They both got in the back. As Moose started off again, Culver yelled at him, "What the hell's wrong?"

"The highway," Moose told them, "the goddamn interstate . . ." Culver and Simmer looked quickly at each other, and then Moose said, "It's gone. Where it was, there ain't hardly nothing."

Simmer took no notice, sitting back as though he were in a taxi. But Culver held himself rigid, his hands and arms dangling over the back of the front seat. "What are you saying?" he said. He was filled with fog and bewilderment.

Moose hit the wheel with his right hand. "I'm telling you they up and left. There's nothing there." He held up a hand that shook a little in the cold air. "You'll see," he finally said. "You'll see for yourself."

The car sped along Route 10 as though the snow under the wheels did not exist, and several times it started into small skids. But the speed alone straightened it out and kept it moving like a rocket toward the interstate.

It was not far, less than a mile, to where Route 10 rose in a little bluff and overlooked the vast expanse of the interstate's path. Moose stopped, and the three of them got out and shuffled the few steps to the side of the road. What they saw was not quite as Moose had said. A first glance showed nothing but a huge concave area that looked as though it had been carefully sculptured out of porcelain. The snow had smoothed out everything and made the hard dug-up areas of the ground symmetrical. Where the tree line had been savaged, there was now the gentle ruffle of a never-ending snowdrift; where the great wheels of the giant bucketloaders had cut huge ruts, there looked to be nothing but the slightest indentation in the snow. In the bright sun that moved quickly between the straggling clouds the whole approach to the valley looked highly polished, as though a wondrous blanket had settled over it all. "See, for Christ's sake," Moose said.

But as Culver and Simmer looked closer they saw where the snow pushed up a little here and there, and they knew that those mounds held the barely concealed bulldozers and graders that only the day before had moved freely over the whole area. Even as they stood there, in the middle of the approach, where the wind blew hardest, a bulldozer's exhaust stack was already beginning to jut above the top of the snow. It looked for a moment like a submarine just beginning to break the surface, and after a few more gusts from the wind the stack was clear and the outline of the cab began to show itself. "We got them," Moose said. "We got them licked."

"It's all there," Culver said to Simmer. "Every last goddamn stitch of it."

"Just waiting."

As they got into the car they all simultaneously saw Sorenson's station wagon creep slowly around the far turn in the road and ease to a stop no more than fifty yards ahead. They watched as he got out of the car and looked over the construction area in the same way they had done. Carrying his left arm across his middle under the heavy coat, he looked like a cartoon drawing of his former self. The position of his arm made him look fifty pounds heavier, and he stood in a strange rigid way, as though constantly trying to balance himself. Only the white ends of the sling stood out at the back of his neck, quivering continually in the hard wind.

They watched as Sorenson glanced at them and then quickly looked back out over the construction site. He stood there for a long time without moving, and only occasionally did his head twitch and snap as if he'd heard a distant gunshot. "What's the bastard doing here?"

Simmer said. He looked for all the world as if he were watching a ghost.

"He's got a right," Culver said, not taking his eyes from Sorenson.

"Straight to hell with him," Moose said, putting his foot down slowly on the gas. As the car gained speed and moved past Sorenson, the man turned, and in a sad way he raised his good hand in what Culver thought for just an instant was a genuine greeting.

Six

They moved Millie's store the second week in January. Where there should have been great joy in the project, there was only a fretful despair, and although not one of them ever mentioned it, they knew it was because already they were a full month behind schedule. Although Culver's plans and organization were nearly flawless, nothing seemed to go right. For days the work crept along, and at almost every significant turn there was some kind of setback. Two days before the concrete workers were to pour the footings and the foundations, the road into the new town thawed into something resembling silly putty. The concrete had to be pumped through long hoses over a distance of nearly a hundred yards. Delay: four days. When the state inspector came to check the septic systems and the leaching fields, he found Culver's and Millie's defective in grade and ordered that they be reconstructed and elevated two and a half feet. When Culver protested to him, he told Culver that Frank Sorenson was a personal friend of his and that the septic systems were, as he put it, "Goddamn well going to be superperfect or they weren't going to be at all." To get done what he ordered took fifty-six loads of gravel fill brought in by three ten-wheeler dump trucks. Delay: four days.

Three of the four wells went in one right after the other, and each time they hit water just before the 200-foot level. But Simmer's well was a huge problem. At 570 feet there was still no water, and when they pulled out and started another hole, one of the crew dropped a hammer down at the hundred-foot level, and it took the bit two days to grind it up before they could go on. Delay: five days. Two thousand-gallon septic tanks cracked as they were being set, a bulldozer cut the septic line from Moose's tank to the leaching field, and the people from the power company said that they would not work when the temperature was twenty degrees or colder. Total delay: nine days. The other eight days of delay were accounted for by the weather itself. The temperature bounced around during those two months in such cycles that the final effect was to unnerve everyone who had anything at all to do with the new town. For two or three days the ground would freeze rock-hard, and wherever a particular crew worked, its progress was painfully slow. Then, as though someone had turned on a giant hot blower, the wind would pick up from the south-south-west and overnight turn most of the town into a layer of soft slick mud. The work went faster then, but the people who did it complained a good deal more.

The only one who did not complain throughout was Culver. He was too intent on his goal to admit that slowly it seemed to be slipping from him. Although he said nothing, that fact registered clearly in his face. As each day came and went Culver appeared diminished, as though in little unseen bits and pieces all of his life's energy were being snatched from him. Where, once, moving most of the important buildings in Oldenfield had been his goal, now it was simply to get Millie's store in place. It was impossible to accomplish anything more than the safe transport of the store; and that was all they cared about.

The morning when they did finally move the store

broke clear and bright. The sun looked warm and full of fresh energy as it lay across the snow in bright yellow heaps. From inside it looked almost like a late spring sun, with the power to heat and melt everything it fell on. But outside, at seven-thirty, the temperature stood at twelve below zero. The sun had no effect on the air temperature, and it felt as if the lovely light from the sun were itself a product of the cold.

When Culver drove up in front of the store, Millie immediately came outside. As though in answer to a question, she said, "It's as ready as it's ever going to be." Moose and Simmer came next. They parked a little way down the road and walked the last few yards to the store. The four of them stood in the bright sunlight like newly formed statues, looking first at each other and then at the store.

Then Culver looked at his watch, and simultaneously Moose said, "The bastards better be sharp." As though it were a cue, the sound of the great flatbed truck came from the bend down near Route 10. There was a fierce roar from the engine and then a metallic grinding of the teeth in the gears as the truck turned and began to heave its way up the little rise toward Millie's store. What was at first utterly stunning about the truck was its size. It looked as if it could have been used as a runway for small planes, and its length clearly dwarfed the store. Millie let out a little gasp, and Moose said, "We could put the whole town on the damned thing."

But even more awesome, and a little frightening to those who watched, was the crane that followed the truck. It sat on its own flatbed surface like a great arrogant bird still asleep. It was stretched out flat, and the huge steel end of it shot out and away from the truck like a deformed beak. From its end hung a silly-looking and quite dirty red flag.

The men went to work with leisurely efficiency. Culver had prepared the foundation himself, and within an hour the store was ready to be hoisted and put on the flatbed truck. The huge cables from the crane hung limply down over the store, and, once attached, they appeared ready at any moment to snap taut on their own. Just before eleven o'clock the crane operator blew the horn in his cab, and within a few seconds Millie's store was several inches off its foundation. Even at so short a distance it swayed just enough to make Millie look away. For an instant she thought that when she looked back she would see her store sailing up and away high over the trees and into the distant sky. In total, the little building never got more than three feet off the ground, and the entire process of loading it onto the flatbed truck took no more than nine or ten minutes. Finally, it sat on the truck square in the middle, and the building itself looked confused and bewildered. And, too, it looked ugly and very old. Sitting where it had in the crease of the little knoll, it had looked right and proper, as though it belonged exactly there and absolutely nowhere else. Now, suddenly, where it had been there was nothing but the dark cellar hole, and the store looked unlike a store, unlike a building. Having been snatched from its setting, it clearly had no value.

At a little before noon the truck pulled away and at a snail's pace began to inch its way up the little rise and past the post office. At the top of the rise the truck turned left and headed out toward the new town. Culver and Moose drove behind the store in Culver's truck, Simmer and Millie following them. "We're doing it," Moose spontaneously volunteered. "We are, by God, doing it."

As the little group moved slowly along the edge of town and then onto the road that went around the lake, Moose every so often slapped his fist into his palm or exclaimed once again that indeed they were doing it.

Had he not been so excited, he would have seen a deep anxiety move over Culver's face in little gray shadows. What Culver saw was the height of the store. With the three feet of the truck, the ten feet of the walls of the store, and the four-foot pitch of the roof, the small one-story building actually took on the height of one twice its size. Culver watched as the house slid in and among the bare tree branches, and when he saw the utility and telephone wires go over the top of the house with only five or six feet to spare, an ugly, sickening weight fell on him.

"Damn straight we're going to do it," Moose said when they were about halfway to the new town.

"Shut up," Culver told him. He was straining his neck to see through the windshield directly above him.

"I could stand a six-pack, all right," Moose said.

"Shut the hell up," Culver said again.

"What's got you?" Moose said. "Here we are, really doing it, and you start foaming at the mouth."

"We may be doing it," Culver said. His head was still turned sharply up. "Getting it done is another thing."

In the car that followed, Millie saw the same thing, and when they finally arrived at the new town she hardly noticed the preparations to move her store onto its new foundation. She went as quickly as she could to Culver. "You can't move the other buildings," she said flatly.

Simmer's and Moose's heads jerked toward her violently. "I know," Culver said quietly. "I saw."

"What the hell you talking about?" Moose shot at her.

"The trees, the wires," she told him. "They're too low for the other buildings."

The faces of the others sagged and went white. When they turned and looked at the store sitting on the truck, they knew that what she was saying was true. "But the wires they can take off and hook back up," Moose said.

"And who's going to cut down a mile and a half of tree limbs?" Culver said. He turned around in very private panic and stared in a sweeping circle about the whole place. The only thing he saw was Sorenson's station wagon parked down by the state road. For just an instant he was certain that he could see Sorenson grinning like hell through the windshield.

Within the next hour they had Millie's store set firmly on the new foundation, and the moving crew was very pleased with its job. They had to shim up just one side of the building, and that by only two and a half inches. Only one of the corners of the foundation, the northeast one, was out of square, but the building was almost ready-made for the error, and by three o'clock the crew was setting the oil burner and the hot water heater. Through it all, Culver stood with the others in a tight little group. There was about them the feeling that the planning had been utterly perfect, that if the other buildings had been one-story a clear and total victory would have easily been theirs. But the presence of Millie's store on its new foundation seemed to give them far more pain than joy, and from time to time it looked as if all four would have been better off if they had left Oldenfield totally intact for the bulldozers. Collectively, they felt a kind of dislocation and despair which they realized came from the simple fact that they themselves had begun to wreck a good part of the town.

The final act of the moving crew was to hook up the power to the little store, which they did just as twilight was grinding out the last of its pale energy in the sky. Inside, the lights went on and the store glowed brightly from every window. To the four of them, what they had done was right, and in their way the lights from the little store affirmed that. The store itself seemed renewed, as though the light that came from it declared a fine new permanence of its own. When the four went into the store, there was the feeling that it once again belonged to them all.

However, that sensation died quickly as Millie said,

"What the hell's going to happen now?" She had assumed her natural place behind the counter, and the expression on her face said clearly that she was very much afraid.

"Nobody under the sun is going to bring a building as big as the post office down that road," Simmer said.

"Nor my house, nor your garage," Culver added.

"It was a good idea," Moose said. "For a baboon." In Moose's face there were deep sad lines of defeat. "You got us into this," he said to Culver. "How could you be so goddamn stupid?"

"Let him alone," Millie said. Culver was looking off somewhere beyond the store and the new woods around the town. Seemingly tuned to a long prayer, he took no notice of anything Moose said.

"And all our money," Moose went on. "Every last cent of it."

"He's out there right now," Culver said. Instantly they knew that he was talking about Sorenson. "And he knows precisely what's happened." He paused and then said, "And he probably knew it long before we did."

Suddenly Moose was viciously angry. He squared himself and faced Culver. "You did this, you know," he said. "You've got to take the responsibility. It's all on you."

"I suppose all along someone's been holding a gun on you," Culver said to him.

"It's you that's done it," Moose said. "It's you that got it in your head to go and save the town."

"You call four buildings and a crossroad saving a town?" Culver shot at him. "If, that is, we ever get them here? I never in my life wanted to save the town. I'm not that stupid." He looked away, and again his eyes seemed to go through the walls and out beyond the town and the fields. "The only thing I ever wanted to save was the idea of the town," he said.

"But you ain't even got that," Moose said.

"Maybe no, maybe yes," Culver answered.

There was a tone in his voice that made Simmer's head snap toward him. "You got something in your head," Simmer said flatly.

"It's the fourteenth of January," Culver said as though he were beginning some long private conversation. "Give or take early thaw, we got us maybe a month, maybe six weeks."

"Until what?" Simmer asked.

"Ice-out," Culver said.

"What the hell does ice-out on Prior Lake have to do with moving three buildings?" Moose said to the whole room.

"Nothing," Culver said, "unless you're going to move the three buildings across that ice."

"You're crazy," Simmer told him.

"No house crew'll go anywhere near it," Moose said.

"We'll do it," Culver said quietly, and then in a sudden burst he added, "For Christ's sake, if I had just one bulldozer and a good length of rope I could do it myself."

"We're beaten," Millie said. "It's lost. All the money, the time, all of it."

"All we've got to do is build the ramps that go down to the lake," Culver said. His eyes were open full and wide, but he saw only what was inside his own mind. His right hand moved down and away from him as though to inscribe the angle of the ramps they would need. Then his left hand rose up in the opposite direction and made the same angle. "Just like that," he said. "I figure maybe seventy-five by fifteen or so."

He looked at Simmer, who shook his head and said, "You'll not get town hall on anything that small."

"*Yards,*" Culver said. "Just so long as we got the houses down to the lake. From there it'd be easy. You could stand behind one and push it with your finger."

"You know how thick the ice is going to have to be?" Moose said.

"Four foot," Culver said. "At four foot you could land jet planes on it."

"It ain't been that all winter," Simmer said.

"The winter isn't over," Culver said.

When it gets cold in the northern parts of New England everything stops dead, and a clearing sky at sunset will send the temperature to inhuman depths. That the cold did come, and come that very night, was clearly a mixed blessing. When they came out of the store to start back to Oldenfield, it was as though the cold were poised and ready to hit with a tremendous force. As they went to their trucks, Moose hollered to Culver, "I'll make it twenty-five below tonight." His breath hung in the moonlight like a small cloud that had been painted on the night.

"It'll be colder than that," Culver yelled back.

By seven o'clock the temperature was already sixteen below. But Culver did not notice the cold, and as he drove back to Oldenfield the vision of the ramps to and from the lake jumped and danced in his mind. Where the others were exhausted from the day, Culver gained strength from the work and the excitement, and when he got back to his house he was neither tired nor hungry. He went to work immediately to calculate what lumber he would have to order in the morning, and several times he found himself wanting to begin the work that night. "Two rotten measurements is all I need," he announced to the empty room. Then, as if to end an argument with himself, he took his coat and went outside. He didn't even try to get to his truck. The first few steps he took were full of energy and determination, and he did not notice the cold. In fact, the first thing he noted was that the night felt a little warmer. It took Culver a few more steps before he realized that the cold was almost an exotic thing that night. It seemed to him that the ordi-

178

nary recognizable world around him had quietly changed in the past several hours. The cold felt for a moment almost like a non-cold, although it had in fact become a real, killing thing. Culver felt it attack him as if he were experiencing some long-faded romance. His senses were almost immediately useless, his reasoning suddenly reduced to a giddy kind of confidence. The air around him became an ether that would not give sleep, and it was only through an involuntary jerking of his body that he found himself turned around and walking the few steps back to his house. When he finally closed the door behind him, he felt an enormous exhaustion, as though the night air had somehow been able to slide under his skin and eat away quickly at the flesh near his bones. In the first faint light of dawn, just before six o'clock, Culver saw that the temperature was forty-one below zero.

They spent the next several days moving Millie's belongings into her store in the new town, and the work gave them a real sense of accomplishment. All except Culver, that is. He was utterly furious at the length of the cold spell, and about all he could contribute to the others was a series of remarks such as, "Nobody could ever drive a sixteen into anything in weather like this. Pine'd be like ice."

The cold did not break at all for three days, and when it did let up, it was not for long. The daytime temperature did not get above ten to twelve degrees below zero, and at night it went consistently to thirty-five below. But Culver used the time well during the cold spell, and when on the eighth day he awoke to gray warm skies and the dripping of icicles from his roof, he was ready. The lumber for the ramps had come two days before and had been stacked in the snow at both ends of the lake at the places where Culver had planned for the buildings to begin and end their trip across the ice.

Culver's plan was simple in all respects except one: the scope of what he intended to do. He had calculated the slope of the ramp that would lead from Route 10 to the lake, and he had predicted almost exactly the amount of lumber needed for the job. None of the technical or abstract parts of the job really presented any difficulty. The only real problem was that the ramp had to be no less than forty-three feet wide—and a little over seventy yards long. The one at the other end of the lake would have to be longer, a shade under eighty yards.

"You know how long this is going to take us?" Moose said the first morning at the site.

"This one'll be about a month," Culver told him, "and that's if the weather's right and good. And the other'll be two, maybe three weeks. The slope of that one's under two degrees. But this bitch"—he pointed to where the ramp would go—"is six and a half degrees."

"That's too steep," Moose told him. "Ain't no building going to take that incline. She'll go down it like a landslide."

"Shut up," Culver answered.

They went to work in a careful and methodical way, as though they would parcel out the entire job in exactly thirty days. The whole area from Route 10 down to the ice was cleared off in five sweeps of the bulldozer, and then they began to grade it carefully. Culver paid special attention to the places where the heaviest supports would go, and as he dug down through the frozen sand he knew that even the slightest thaw at the wrong time would mean immediate disaster. But in his mind he could see everything as it should be in the end, and that vision kept him full of energy and in charge of every detail. His absorption in the job was complete, and on the third morning of work Moose had to shout at him several times to get him to look up to where Sorenson's station wagon was parked on Route 10. "What the hell's he want?" Moose called to Culver.

Culver raised his hand as though to quiet Moose but he fixed his gaze on the station wagon. From where he stood he had a good view of Sorenson, and what he saw startled him. The man inside the car clearly was Sorenson, but he looked as though he had shriveled a great deal; the coat he wore looked far too big for him. He seemed sad and lost as he sat in the car, and Culver wondered for a moment why Sorenson was looking not at him or at any of the work he and Moose were doing but straight ahead through the windshield at something far, far down the road.

"You want me to run him the hell off?" Moose called.

"Leave him," Culver said. "He's got a right."

Indeed, it was as if Sorenson knew that he had a right to be where he was. Every morning he was at the site a little after nine o'clock, and he left and came back with a regularity that implied he had become one of those working on the ramps. But never did anyone see him watching the progress of the work, and after two weeks they simply accepted him as a fact of the place.

The progress of the first ramp was just as Culver had predicted, and by the end of the second week all the supports for it were tightly in place. From the lake the project looked like a bizarre hurdle race. The supports near the lake were low and squat, but then they rose up like ever more formidable barriers as they marched toward Route 10. It was, as Culver said, "a snug job; the whole thing's probably not off more than a quarter of an inch." When Simmer put the transit to it, he found it to be off by three-quarters of an inch. "It'll take you thirty more years before you'll be a real carpenter," Simmer told him.

"We plank for a week solid," Culver said, "and this'll be done."

They went at the planking with a secure and steady rhythm. Simmer and Moose began at the end down near the lake; Culver started alone at the top of the ramp. Each day they parceled out exactly one-fifth of the work, and always it was done just around four-fifteen in the afternoon. They seemed to be working by some secret inner clock they had been born with. The sounds of the hammers rose and fell with a rhythm so consistent that it seemed at any moment the sound would become a melody. When they broke for lunch, none of them had to look at his watch to know it was time. For the first three and a half days, it was as if the inner workings of their bodies told them when to work and when to eat, and they obeyed without a thought.

But during the afternoon of the fourth day, just as they went back to work after lunch, the weather began to change. From the other end of the lake a warm and gentle wind began to blow. There was a soft and hazy sun in the gray sky, and it gave heat to the breeze that came across the lake. The wind blew steadily for almost two hours, and then, as though controlled by something beyond the lake, it began to come in fragrant puffs. It was when the wind died down and stopped completely that Culver turned from his kneeling position and looked out at the lake. He did not like what he saw. For a moment his eyes swept the whole surface, and then as though in conclusion he sat down on the ramp and pulled his knees to his chest.

The lake was beginning to heat up. From all over it he could see small snatches of mist begin to rise up. He knew that, quite simply, the ice was beginning to melt, and as he sat there the little clouds of steam gathered together to form a light fog just dense enough to obscure the other end of the lake.

Just as Culver was rising up to get a good view, Simmer and Moose saw what was happening. But they seemed more concerned with Culver's face than with the condition of the ice, and it was Simmer who yelled, "Pay it no mind."

But Culver did not hear him. He stood like some silly captain on the bridge of an equally silly ship, and the only thing that made him appear at all serious was the look of utter hate that had spread across his face. Suddenly, as though in response to a silent statement from the lake itself, Culver raised his hammer and shouted, "I don't give a goddamn what you do, those houses are going across you."

Almost in answer to Culver came the first audible crack in the ice. It was not so much a crack as it was the sound of a thousand knuckles snapping all at once. When Moose and Simmer heard it, they looked first at each other and then directly at Culver. They watched him turn away and drop back to his knees, and they continued to watch him as he began again to drive the nails into the planks. There was a fierce determination in the way the hammer struck the heads of the nails, as though the follow-through of the hammer were strong enough to go right on through the wood itself.

"We got us maybe two weeks," Moose said as he looked out over the lake.

"At the outside," Simmer said.

Two weeks was just exactly right, and the race to finish the ramp at the other end of the lake was feverish. During the first few days of work on it the warm mellow air still streamed out of the southwest and blew with a steady energy over the mountains and down across the lake. On the third day Culver knew that unless somehow the work could go faster, the ice would be too weak to sustain the buildings. That was when he rigged the lights so that he could work into the night. At first he worked alone, with only the lights of his truck to help him see where the nails were to go. Simmer joined him on the night of the fifth day, and Moose, with two huge spotlights, finally came back after dinner the next night. Because of the cold, they did not make much headway working at night, and more than anything else it served to keep them from thinking what would happen if they did not beat the ice. Although the heavy cold snaps were over for the winter, the temperature still sank into the teens soon after dark. The effect was to make their work appear as though they were caught in slow motion. Even though they swung their hammers with the same controlled force as in daylight, there was a diminished effect when the hammer hit home. It was almost as though the wood they worked with had begun to freeze, the juices in it drying up to rock-hard at the moment the sun went out of the sky.

But the night work did make a difference, and on the ninth day Culver looked at the ramp and pronounced that in three days at the most they would be ready.

"It looks like we're going to have a shot at it," Moose said.

"Weather's got to hold," Simmer said as though to himself.

"We've beaten it," Culver said. "We're going to do it." He flipped the hammer into the air beside his head, and it spun around several times very fast. When it dropped, Culver thrust out his hip at just the precise moment, and the hammer dropped handle first through the metal ring of the holster at his belt. With a little metallic click it snapped into place all by itself. The three of them stood for a moment with their faces alive for the first time in what seemed almost years.

"By God," Simmer started to say with great energy, but he never finished the sentence. From above them on the road came the shrill honking of Millie's horn. The three of them turned to see her waving frantically at them. Together they scrambled up the ramp and hurried the last few feet to the road. Culver was the first to get to her. She looked almost close to death. "Black ice," she said, without looking at him.

"*No!*" Culver said with such force that Millie's head snapped back a little.

"Oh, Christ, where?" Moose asked.

"I counted maybe three places," Millie answered. "Two for sure."

"Show me," Culver demanded. The three of them were in the jeep and moving off down the road as though they had all just heard the fire siren scream out across the valley. From a little rise a mile down the road they were all able to see the two patches of black ice not more than fifty yards apart. Culver scanned the lake with his hands cupped at each temple as though he held binoculars. "It looks all right," he said. "The rest of it looks solid." In his mind he could see the frigid boiling of the two small jetlike streams shooting up from the lake bottom just under the patches of black ice. And he saw in his mind hundreds of others all over the four miles of the lake, working away in their own private icy darkness at the underside of the ice. They told him that the snow cover even on the highest parts of the mountain was beginning to melt and run off into the underground feeder streams for the lake. Finally, he turned around in the jeep and looked at Simmer and Moose. "We go in two days," he said to them.

"It can't be done," Moose told him.

"Shut up," Culver said. He turned very slowly and looked back out at the lake. "And everything goes at once."

"Goddamn it," Simmer said.

"Everything," Culver said. "Your place, my place, the post office and town hall. It all goes in two days."

"One at a time'll be tough enough," Millie said. She looked at Culver hard.

"All of it at the same time," Moose said, "just can't be done. There ain't no way."

Again Culver whipped around from the front seat and said, "Twenty telephone poles, four abreast, each five feet apart." He put out his hand and spread his four fingers. "Like this," he said. "Then each length is five poles long. We set the buildings on that, like a sled."

"What about overhang?" Simmer asked.

"To hell with it," Culver said and turned around again.

"You know what our chances are?" Simmer said.

"I do," Culver answered quietly.

"And what you got them figured at?"

"Maybe one in ten."

"Well, I'm staying put," Simmer told him. He sat back in his seat and folded his arms tightly across his chest.

Again Culver spun around, and for a long moment he looked at Simmer. "Not on your life," he said. "You're going to do it and you're going to like doing it." He threw his hand in the air. "So we don't make it. So what? I don't give a goddamn. That's not the important thing." Then his voice evened off and settled in a soft way throughout the whole jeep. "The only thing that's important is trying to do it," he said.

"I don't want my garage at the bottom of the lake."

"Then you can put pontoons on it and paddle it across," Culver said.

"Both of you shut up, for God's sake," Millie said.

"Either you're in or you're out," Culver told Simmer.

"In," Simmer answered and looked away. Across the lake the sun was sliding into a soft notch between two hills, and for a few minutes its red melting in the sky made it look like a mind suddenly gone berserk.

The next two days were frenzied with activity, and the weather again complicated the final preparations. It became downright warm, and that fact pushed the men ahead with a terrific flurry of energy. They could see the lake clearly beginning to come alive as the patterns of black ice began to spread in a kind of random selection throughout the whole lake. Culver drove the length of the lake that day, and although the top few inches of ice had melted into a slick covering of water, he saw that the surface was strong and even. When he got back to Moose and Simmer he proudly announced that the ice was fit for travel.

"It just ain't going to work," Simmer said, and, turning away from the other two, he began to nail together the supports and crossbeams that would hold the telephone poles.

At just after four o'clock the next afternoon they were ready. The ramps at either end of the lake sat like great flat arms, and the giant sled of telephone poles and planking sat on the edge of the ice as if it had been moored there forever. But there was no joy in any of them, and where there should have been a sense of accomplishment, there was only a mounting fear. It was as though they had finished everything they knew how to do, and that what stood before them now possessed an unknown quality. During that day a kind of unspoken terror had crept into each of their faces. As they broke up to go to their houses to finish the final preparations, they did not speak. As they left the site of the ramps each man looked over the work they had all done. They were suddenly caught in small little worlds. Until he was in his car, Moose kept his hammer loosely in his hand, as if at any moment he might be called upon to use it once again. As Simmer went off to his truck he carried himself like a man in deep grief, and every few steps he shook his head slowly. Culver watched them both go, and then with one final glance over the whole area he began to climb the ramp toward his truck. When he got to the top he turned and looked back once again. There was a clear pride in his face as he looked at the giant sled, and in his mind he could see the buildings proudly sitting on it, ready at last to go to the new town.

But as his gaze trailed out and over the lake, his face sagged and his eyes narrowed down into little slits. What he suddenly realized so deeply in his soul that he felt instantly sick was that very probably the whole plan would not work. In quick little flashes he saw the houses crashing down through the ice, suspended for a few moments like some bizarre flotilla, and then inch by inch sinking out of sight forever.

As he stood there, suddenly it felt like the whole world was coming apart. The explosion he heard sounded as if some giant bomb had gone off at the far end of Oldenfield. There was initially a terrific blast that reached Culver with a deafeningly sharp sound that vibrated in his ears long after the explosion was over. The sound careened out and over the lake, and for what seemed several minutes Culver heard it bounce itself out among the nearby hills.

No sooner was that explosion lost in the distance than another took its place. The second one was so powerful that it seemed to feed off the first. Culver's immediate reaction was to start for his truck, but when the third explosion hit, he froze where he was. In the next instant he was afraid for Millie and Moose and Simmer and for all the buildings still left in the town. He felt as if a huge section of the world were being removed, and it was with great effort that he got into his truck and headed off down Route 10.

The explosions were now nearing ten in number and coming faster and faster. In the truck it was not possible for Culver to say which of the great sounds was the explosion and which the echo. They all melted into one continuous roar of super-thunder.

It was from a little rise just on the edge of town near the cemetery that Culver saw the reason for the explosions. The interstate was already there. In one incredible leap it had risen up like some giant uncoiling snake and flung itself forward nearly a quarter of a mile. The path had been cut through an enormous rock formation several hundreds of feet high in so precise a way that it looked sculptured. Where the stakes had once stood in the thinned-out woods, they were now the only things that jutted up from the muddy snow cover. They appeared to Culver to be holding back the woods that stood tense and weak just behind them.

In the middle of the whole area, not more than a hundred yards from the severed rock formation, was Sorenson's station wagon. Behind it several men in parkas and yellow hard hats huddled around the detonators as though warming themselves by a fire. Culver turned away from them and looked through the back window of the cab. What he saw snapped into clear and sharp focus all the events of the past year. Between the highway and the town there was now only one final stand of birch trees. For a moment they looked to Culver like lovely lacy fingers rising up from the ground in pure fear.

Through the stand of trees the town of Oldenfield was just barely visible. Culver saw the main street curling up toward the post office, the top edge of Simmer's Garage, and just the barest outline of the turn in the road that led to his own house. For just an instant the misty outline of the town looked strange to him. It was as though he had lived there only in a dream, as if the whole town were already gone and only ghost and shadow images of it remained. He suddenly felt an intense longing to be away from the town, to reject it, to be in the new town among new trees in the fresh spring air.

The next morning they took Culver's house first, and it was a disaster almost from the beginning. The moving crew was the same one that had moved Millie's store, and they were none too happy about loading three buildings onto a ramp and sliding them down some seventy-five yards to the lake. Culver had gotten them to agree to it, but the attitude of the six men on the crew was that they were working on a job run by crazy people. In a way, Culver was the super-foreman of the job, and all throughout the first part of securing the house and then moving it to the flatbed truck he was everywhere giving instructions to the crane operator. But his instructions were ignored, and when he tried to block the first effort to lift the house because of the way a cable had been improperly secured, he was told by the crane operator to go to hell. The result was that the cable snapped with a great whiplike sound, and then as though it were made of elastic it curled up and whipped around the very top of the crane. The house lurched slowly to the left, and for a moment it appeared that it would shrug out of its wire sling and tumble over on its side. But it did not. The crane operator got it to rest just on the edge of the foundation, and as though he were playing with toys he balanced it there. Culver watched the whole thing, and when he was certain that the house was secured, he turned and went to Simmer's truck. As he got in, Simmer looked at him and said, "Christ's sake, you all right?"

Culver's face looked gray and full of ashes. "This could be the greatest day of my life," he answered. After a few moments he got hold of himself, and finally he said, "Let's get us the hell out of here. We can wait it out at the ramp."

They drove away from the house and down along the main street of the town at a very slow speed. It was as though each of them were giving it one last look, and from the activity at the other end of the town they knew that the buildings that would stay behind would be lying in their own ruins within hours. The bulldozers from the interstate were clearing away the last stand of birch, and with each passing second the vast space that would become the highway inched nearer. Then suddenly they saw two of the bulldozers come shoulder to shoulder and gun forward through the final thin line of trees. The trees fell as though whipping themselves to the ground as fast as they could. Then everything changed before their eyes. Where the town had dominated the whole immediate area, now the path for the highway took over in importance, and its scope and depth were so impressive that it made the town look grossly insignificant, completely humbled. It looked as if in no way did it belong where it was, as though the buildings were silly primitive things that would at any given second turn and flee into the deeper woods.

Behind the bulldozers Sorenson walked majestically, as though he understood the machines to be his private escorts. As Culver and Simmer approached the little bend in the road, Sorenson held up his hand and Simmer eased the truck to a stop. Culver and Simmer stared at Sorenson as he came up to Simmer's side of the truck. With one finger raised he beckoned Simmer to roll down the window. "You must know," Sorenson said, "that the town will be razed by tomorrow." His left hand, or what was left of it, was in a little black sack tied at his wrist. He held the hand across his chest as if it had grown there. "Perhaps even by this afternoon," he said. He looked away from the truck and up toward the road by the post office where Culver's house was just beginning to creep around the turn. "The ice will never hold it," he said.

"Then I'll get a stick and part the waters," Culver said.

Culver's house went down the ramp and onto the giant sled with such ease that even Culver was startled by it. The winches at the top of the ramp worked perfectly, and the cables attached to the house played out with an even perfection. There was no trouble at all except where the sled met the ramp. The angle there was too sharp to allow the front part of the house to slide easily onto the sled, and Culver had to start the bulldozer and bring it up on the left rear corner of the building. With one soft push he brought the blade against the corner, and the building slipped the necessary several inches. As it settled onto the far end of the sled, Culver looked at it with a mixture of triumph and fear. In little places all around the front end of the sled the top few inches of ice were splintering and shattering from the weight. Culver watched it closely, and in a few seconds the process stopped, as though the ice had made its effort to accommodate the weight and had won.

The post office came next, barely making it from the flatbed truck to the top of the ramp. The clearance between the tops of the trees and the roof of the post office was literally two or three inches, and as the crane held the huge building poised at the top of the ramp, Culver told Simmer to get his chain saw and start to work on the tree that by itself formed a canopy near the top of the ramp. "If we're going to take the town hall," he told Simmer, "it's got to come down."

Simmer stood for a moment and looked at it. His gaze moved back and forth between it and the post office at the top of the ramp. "Ain't no way to cut that one," he finally told Culver, "and not have it smack in the middle of the ramp."

"Put a line to it," Culver said, "and hook it to the 'dozer."

"It ain't going to work," Simmer said again. With his hand he outlined the awkward shape of the tree and how it had all grown over toward the side nearest the ramp.

"I don't give a goddamn," Culver said. "Cut the son of a bitch down."

The winches whined out their lines as the post office began to inch its way down the ramp. As Culver watched he saw the building move in reality exactly as it had in his mind. The cables that secured it vibrated hard, as if in tune with some unheard song of pure raw strength. Just when the building got to the end of the ramp, Culver again had to nudge the edge of it onto the sled. But when it was fully on, it slid slowly and with almost no effort into its position just behind Culver's house. As Culver began to place the pegs that secured the building to the sled, he heard again the brief cracking of the ice. When he looked down he saw where the side of the sled was beginning to make a slight imprint in the ice.

It was then that Culver heard the sharp sound of the chain saw, and he looked up just in time to see Simmer thrust the blade rudely into the thick trunk of the tree. Back beyond the tree he saw Moose sitting on the bulldozer, the line from it to the tree taut and rigid. He watched for a few moments as the sound of the saw hummed into the middle of the trunk. Then as he looked away to where Sorenson's station wagon was pulling up, he heard the saw stop as Simmer yelled to Moose, "Pull, goddamn it. She's going to go."

It was almost a comedy of confusion. Moose threw the gears on the bulldozer, which lurched ahead and started across the road. The cable to the tree snapped like a piece of melodic twine, and then the tree began to ease forward in the direction of the ramp. It fell in what began as beautiful slow motion and ended in a great swift roar. The sound it made as the top part of it hit the ramp was a crunching ugly thing, a sound that seemed a good deal more vicious and fearful than it actually was. Then throughout the whole place there was a stillness that shut off even the gentle rustlings of the wind.

After a few more minutes Culver walked up the ramp and began to survey the damage. He was surprised that only two of the supports were broken, and when he looked up and waved to Simmer and Moose they came immediately. "You two start clearing," he told them, and instantly Simmer began to work on the tree, and Moose pulled the limbs away as quickly as Simmer sliced them off. Culver climbed over the other parts of the tree and walked slowly up to Sorenson's car. "I don't want any of your crap," he said. "All I want is your saw."

"Help yourself," Sorenson answered. He gestured toward the rear of the station wagon. "I'd be the last one in the world to stop you now."

"That tree'll be cleared inside an hour."

"No building as big as that town hall will go down that ramp," Sorenson said flatly.

"I built that ramp," Culver said. He took the saw from its case, and as he held it for a moment he said, "What're you always hanging around for?"

"That's my business," Sorenson answered.

"If you're waiting for us to fail," Culver said, "you're in for a long wait."

"No," Sorenson said.

"Then *what?*" Culver threw at him.

"I'm here because you need me."

"Like a hole in the head," Culver said. He turned and started down toward Moose and Simmer.

The ramp was cleared within the hour, but the effort took a great deal out of the three of them. Simmer and Moose were more affected than Culver, and when the town hall rode through the tree line near the top of the ramp like some ghostly castle, only Culver was revived by the sight. Simmer and Moose stood off to one side of the ramp in a hunched-over way, as though the effort of clearing the tree had taken from them all their final strength.

The town hall slid down the ramp in a series of spastic little jerks, and as soon as the first one shuddered through the building, Culver realized that the winches were slipping. He also realized that there was absolutely nothing he could do about it. He stood at his spot near the bottom, his eyes shifting from the huge building to Sorenson and then back again. At the precise moment that the building passed above the broken supports, it seemed that the winches simply gave up. The huge building slid sideways and over the damaged area, and just as it looked as though it would hurtle the rest of the way down the ramp, the winch lines caught again and the building bumped and lurched for a few more feet before once again it came under control.

When it was finally parked on the sled, Culver turned the bulldozer so he could get a clear view of Sorenson. He saw that a transformation had come over him, that where there had been a silly pleased look on his face, there was now the appearance of disbelief and horror. "The bastard never thought we could do it," Culver yelled to Simmer and Moose. Culver turned back and raised his arm in Sorenson's direction. Then half in triumph and half in anger he shook his fist so hard that the rest of his body appeared to vibrate with it.

Within the next hour they had Simmer's Garage secured to the back of the sled, and when Simmer complained that the overhang might unbalance the whole thing, Culver told him that there was so much weight on the sled that the Empire State Building wouldn't make the slightest difference now. Simmer looked at Culver and then at the sled. "When do we go?" he asked.

"Now," Culver said.

"You know there ain't enough light," Simmer told him.

"I know the ice here won't hold this thing for more than an hour or so," Culver said. Almost as though in answer, an ugly sound came from under the sled. It was as though the sound were actually from some huge wounded person. For a moment Culver and Simmer were afraid of it. When it happened again they looked down to see the little slivers of white spreading out from under the sides of the sled. Several feet below the surface the hard ice was beginning to break up. Then came a series of little cracking sounds, like distant pistol shots, and every so often, punctuating them, the groaning came.

Without so much as a word between them, Culver turned from Simmer and climbed back on his bulldozer. He drove it slowly around in front of the sled, backed it in carefully, and then waited for Simmer to come and hook the cable to the back of the bulldozer. When it was secured, Simmer turned and waved for Moose, and when he finally came down the ramp they both moved out ahead of the bulldozer by twenty yards or so.

As they walked across the ice about thirty feet apart, their eyes never looked up even for an instant. When they were almost fifty yards from Culver they turned and looked back at him. Then Simmer put both his hands over his head and with a quick whipping motion ordered Culver to come ahead.

The bulldozer immediately burst into life. The black smoke spat quickly from the exhaust stack, and the engine declared its great power in a series of whines and moans. Simmer motioned again with his arms, and at the same instant the bulldozer's front end rose up a few inches from the ice; then, like some exotic train leaving its berth, the bulldozer and sled ground forward several feet. All around, the ice snapped and cracked as the teeth on the two tracks crunched into the ice. On the sled the buildings shuddered and swayed a little, but then they seemed to lend their weight to a forward motion, and Culver waved his hand as he felt the bulldozer finally gain complete control over its load.

Simmer and Moose held their ground and watched as Culver came toward them at no more than a half-mile an hour. Finally, when Culver waved them on, they both turned and once again began to search the ice for the deep cracks and gray places they all knew were there. When either of them suspected that the ice was treacherous, they waved Culver to one side or the other, and with an easy control he guided the bulldozer and sled to a safer path.

They went on that way for the better part of an hour, and then when the light began to fade into ghostly purples and pinks, Simmer raised his hands and motioned Culver to stop. It took nearly two hundred yards for Culver to bring the momentum of the huge sled under control and to a stop, and when he did so, he immediately heard the ice under him twinge and snap.

"I can't see anymore," Simmer told him. "Everything looks the same." Under him, far below the top of the ice, he heard a huge snapping sound, and for a moment he looked down as though he expected to find himself about to slip out of sight.

"I can't let this thing just sit here," Culver yelled. "If I don't keep it moving, it'll go through inside half an hour." He reached out and put on the headlights, and both of them watched as Culver lowered the blade and the lights sprang out and flooded the ice ahead. "I got to keep her moving," he told Simmer again.

Simmer looked from Culver to Moose, and then he shouted for Moose to take a path slightly to the right. "Over that way a little more," he directed. Then he turned back to Culver and said, "I'll go for the lights." Before Culver could answer him he had slipped away from the bulldozer and was lost in the shadows.

Culver immediately started the engine, and with Moose just barely visible in the headlights, he began once again to creep across the ice. Culver watched Moose scurry back and forth ahead of him, his arms in an almost constant motion as he directed Culver first this way and then that. Culver alternately watched Moose and the fading twilight as it first outlined the soft hills on the horizon and then finally erased them completely.

Within no more than twenty minutes Culver saw Simmer's truck coming across the ice toward him. The bright cones of the headlights swayed back and forth as the truck skidded and fishtailed along the ice. With great precision and timing Simmer moved the truck into position alongside Culver's bulldozer. Then he leaned out the window and said, "It's gone." Culver snapped his head toward him, and Simmer yelled again, "The whole town's gone, right down to my pumps and flagpole."

"Did you think he'd take it board by board?" Culver said.

"But there's just nothing there, not even rubble. It's just a wide space all bladed off."

Simmer eased his foot onto the gas and moved out from Culver and toward where Moose was. He handed Moose a huge flashlight, and Culver was relieved when he saw that it was powerful enough to light the whole area ahead.

A little after midnight the weather began to change. It was Culver who noticed it first. Just when it seemed to him that the night should be turning into its deepest cold, there came an easy breeze from the south. It was a gentle billowy thing, at first like a warm blanket of fur across the face, and then after a few more minutes it picked up and buffeted Culver and the buildings that sat on the sled behind him. By three o'clock the stars were gone from the sky and great gray clouds hunched themselves down over the whole lake. By first light a thin misty rain had settled in, and with it came fluffy patches of fog as the warm rain mixed uneasily with the hard cold of the ice.

Through the mist Culver was able to make out the far end of the lake and the ramp. He estimated that he was about half a mile away. At that same instant Simmer saw the other end too, and he hit his horn twice and motioned to Culver. Culver raised his hand slightly in acknowledgment, and then as his eyes settled back onto the path in front of him a great terror shot through his whole body.

The rain was beginning to turn the whole lake into one huge patch of black ice. Instantly he knew two things. One was that certainly by midmorning the ice would no longer be able to support the bulldozer, let alone the load it pulled. The other thing was that it would not be possible to see where the truly weak places were in the ice ahead. The rain was blending it all into one grayish-black mass.

Culver yelled for Moose to come back to the bulldozer, and then with a gesture of his hand he got Simmer to slow his truck. Moose climbed up into the cab and sat next to Culver. "No use in walking right into it," Culver told him.

"What do you figure we got to go?" His eyes were fixed on the ice ahead.

"Hour, hour and a half," Culver answered.

"You going to take her straight in?"

"Straight in," he said. "We're only just guessing anyway."

Culver lifted his eyes from the ice and looked ahead to where the ramp climbed out of the water and slid quietly toward the road that led to the new town. He could just make out in the gray morning the slim outline of Sorenson's car. Sorenson stood next to it like a shrunken black beetle. "Can you see him?" Culver asked Moose.

"When will the son of a bitch leave us alone?"

Culver was just starting to speak when he heard the ugly crunching sound just behind him. Before he had a chance to turn around and see what it was, he felt a great shudder run through the bulldozer. Even the controls under his hands shook, and then he felt for a moment as though he were being pulled backward by a force over which he had absolutely no control. "Oh, Christ, *no,*" he yelled.

Instantly Moose sprang down from the cab and looked at the sled. "It's going in, it's going in," he yelled to Culver. "Gun it, gun it!"

Culver tried to accelerate, but the only effect it had was to balance for a moment the great weight of the sled. For a few more seconds the grinding of the bulldozer held the sled where it was, and Culver was able to turn around a little to look at what had happened.

What he saw almost made him sick. The rear end of the sled was as firmly set into the ice as if it had been stuck there for years. The water from the lake was over the end of the sled by nearly a foot, and Culver watched it for a second or two as it splashed a little on the side of the garage. The cable from the bulldozer to the sled was so taut that Culver thought he could see its strength diminishing with every passing second. He whipped around and again gave full power to the bulldozer.

At first the machine moved forward a little, but then an utter despair set in, and the bulldozer actually rose up from the ice as though the machine itself finally understood its own uselessness. In the next instant Culver looked up to see Simmer running toward them as fast as he could. "Goddamn it," he was screaming, "I told you, I told you."

Culver turned to Moose. "Is it holding?"

"Barely," Moose said.

Very slowly Culver eased off on the power until the machine once again came under his control. Each time he felt the engine slacken, he expected to find himself hurtling backward directly into the lake. But the sled and the bulldozer were locked together in a huge balance, neither capable of pulling the other. "I told you," Simmer was still saying as he finally came alongside the bulldozer.

"You told me," Culver answered quietly.

"What the hell are you going to do?"

"Get another 'dozer," Culver told him.

"Christ, there ain't no time," Moose said. He looked down to the ice next to the sled, where a bright silver crack wriggled out from under the sled and then like some grotesque dying snake hurled itself back under it. "The whole goddamn thing's going to go," Moose said.

"Go get my sledge," Simmer said to Moose.

"What do you think you're going to do?" Culver asked.

But Simmer did not answer him. The whole sled suddenly sank downward and several feet to the back. The force of it jerked the bulldozer back, and almost instinctively Culver jumped free of it. Together he and Simmer moved back from it. The front end of the sled was now completely off the ice, and the whole thing looked as though at any moment it would flip itself straight back and fling the bulldozer over its head and far down the lake. An enormous tension prevailed, but it seemed as if it had already resolved itself and all that was left was to wait for the sled to go into the lake. But over the next few moments it did not move. It seemed held in place by a strength greater than what the bulldozer itself could supply. It looked, in fact, as though it had been caught and held by some giant will power, some indescribable energy that was at once wondrous and terrifying.

"What are you going to do with the sledge?" Culver asked again.

Moose brought it to Simmer and then stepped back several yards.

"So I'll build a new garage," Simmer said as he snapped the sledgehammer from Moose's hands. "A fine new place," he said, more to himself than to anyone else. He pulled himself up on the sled, and as he began to pick his way back toward the end he yelled to Culver, "When I cut her loose, you gun it."

"Get down off there," Culver yelled.

"It's all the chance there is," Simmer said and turned away.

Culver moved quickly to the bulldozer and once in the seat carefully held the controls under a light firm grip. He heard Simmer begin to hit the sturdy wooden pegs on the back of the sled. There were six of them neatly placed at an angle to the side of the building, and Simmer began to break them off one by one with barely more than a half swing of the sledgehammer.

From where Culver sat he had a clear view of the end of the lake, the ramp, and Sorenson standing next to his station wagon. He looked and then looked again as he saw Sorenson wave at him in a frantic way. Then he saw Sorenson cup his right hand around his mouth to shout. But what he said carried no strength, and the sound died out completely before it was even halfway to Culver.

"Get ready!" Moose yelled. "He's going to hit the last two."

Simmer only barely got to the next peg. As it snapped off cleanly at its base, there was a second or two when everything was in suspension. And then with a quick vicious snap the other pin gave way under the huge weight of the building.

Simmer never really had any chance at all. There was just enough time for him to turn on the back of the sled and move quickly along the planks for several steps. That saved him from being crushed under the building as it slid in, but it did not save him from going into the water. He went in on his side, the motion of his body taking him away from the building but out and several yards under the ice.

When Culver felt the building begin to slide off the sled, he snapped full power to the bulldozer. There was a moment of incredible strain, and then the machine and sled went forward in a great shuddering slide. Culver did not hear Moose's screams as he powered the bulldozer and sled almost thirty yards down the ice. When he looked up from the controls, he was horrified to see Sorenson running across the ice as fast as he could go.

Hanging from his right hand was a loose coil of rope. At that moment Culver turned in the cab and saw Moose waving hysterically. Then he veered the bulldozer sharply, and even before it stopped he was off it and running back to the huge open space in the ice where Simmer's Garage floated half in and half out of the water. There was no sign of Simmer, and even before Culver could speak Moose said, "The whole thing fell on him."

Moose's face was a gray dead color. Culver's eyes swept the grotesque scene in front of him, and then in little ever-widening circles they swept over the ice for some sign of Simmer. Then two things happened at once: Simmer suddenly appeared floating face down no more than two feet from the garage, and they heard Sorenson screaming, "A line—get him a line!"

In the next few minutes both Culver and Moose were frozen where they stood. Culver watched Sorenson's approach as though he were looking at an attraction in a supernatural sideshow. Sorenson suddenly appeared transformed into a sleek, powerful athlete, and as he came toward the water there was a sureness and power to the way he ran. But that picture of him was suddenly shattered as the ice under him gave way a good twenty feet before he thought it would. The ice broke quickly, like a windowpane with a rock going through it, but before Sorenson started to fall, there was a brief instant when he appeared actually to take several quick little steps on top of the water. Then in a great cruel flash he was in and then under it.

"Rope—you got any rope?" Culver yelled at Moose. Moose turned and looked at him hopelessly. "For Christ's sake, you got *anything?*" Culver screamed. Moose's face only turned more sour and hopeless.

Culver snapped his head back and saw that, if anything, Sorenson had taken charge of the situation. He surfaced within twenty feet of Simmer and with easy and powerful strokes he got to him quickly. He yanked Simmer's head out of the water and turned him so he could see his face. It was then that Simmer gave a hard spastic jerk, and both his hands reached out and around Sorenson's neck.

But Sorenson was too quick for him. Instantly he ducked under Simmer's grasp and then after a second or two surfaced behind him. Sorenson grabbed Simmer across the chest, and then, just as he turned a little on his side to begin to swim with him, Simmer went instantly stiff in the water. At first he rose up a little, and then as though being pushed from underneath he came to a grotesque attention pose.

Culver knew precisely what had happened. The cold of the thirty-three-degree water had hit Simmer like a blackjack, and as he stood watching he knew that neither of them would now last more than a few minutes. He saw Simmer pivot slowly next to Sorenson, and the two of them bobbed in slow motion.

"Get to the building!" Culver shouted. "Grab the building!" he screamed, pointing in a futile silly way at the slowly sinking garage.

"Oh, Christ," Moose said. "Somebody do something." He turned away from the horror in front of him and began to walk aimlessly toward the center of the lake. Culver shot his gaze from Simmer and Sorenson to Moose and then back again. He looked for a moment as though he were trying to decide between them. Then finally he went forward toward the black water and began to take off his coat. Under him he could feel the ice sag and groan a little.

"*No!*" Simmer shouted at him. With what appeared almost certainly to be his last bit of strength, he thrust one hand above his head and waved Culver back. "You can't do nothing," Simmer called.

As though in affirmation the ice around Culver again became elastic. He moved back the few steps he had gone, and his hands fell away from the opening of his jacket and hung down limp and foolish at his sides. He watched as Simmer's face almost instantly turned blue, and his eyes closed up slowly and yet with great speed. In a strange rigid motion he leaned out and away from Sorenson, drifted a little toward the middle of the water, and then was gone beneath the surface.

In the next few moments Culver appeared to go completely insane. He opened his jacket and put his hands on his hips. Then he tried to assume a pose with his body that would make him look like a more important person. But he looked absurd, like a street-corner orator gone fully berserk. Finally he exploded in an anger so intense that it threatened literally to consume him. "You son of a bitch," he yelled at Sorenson, "I know what you're doing." He saw a thin weak smile crease Sorenson's mouth. "You're cheating me," Culver hollered. The smile infuriated him all the more. "We'll make it, damn you. You know we will."

"Without me," Sorenson said in a weak voice, "you wouldn't have gotten half of it done."

Culver started forward as though now he would fight him, but then he abruptly stopped and stared. Sorenson rose up a little in the water, and then he said in a soft, private voice, "Help me—please help me."

Culver stood like a man who's been shot and has only just begun to realize it. Sorenson began to lose control of his body, and for a few seconds he thrashed about pathetically. Then his eyes rolled back in his head, and for just an instant he shook violently. As he sank his eyes stayed flipped over as though he were for the first time seeing into himself.

Culver moved back and away from the open area in the ice in a fearful way, and none too soon. Simmer's Garage began almost immediately to shudder and bob in a final anger, and after only a few seconds it heaved on its side and then with no sound at all settled into the lake. Then the whole area of the black water was clear except for occasional huge white bubbles of foam that erupted in the middle of it.

Culver walked backward all the way to where he had left the bulldozer and sled, and he did not turn around until he heard Moose's pathetic sobs. Moose was leaning against the bulldozer. His whole trunk heaved back and forth, and his head snapped from side to side as though in disbelief over all he had seen. Culver went up to him and put an arm across his shoulders. "There's not much time left," he said. "The ice is starting to break up all over." For just a moment he pulled Moose to him, and the two of them stood like old lovers. "You go on ahead," Culver said.

"I go with you."

"I don't know if it'll make it," Culver said.

"I hope it don't."

As Culver moved off, he could feel the ice under the bulldozer and sled become weaker with each passing second. Every so often he felt the bulldozer and sled lean slightly to one side or the other. Moose slowly regained control of himself, and his involuntary groans and half sobs began to ease off. Finally, as though it were an afterthought, he said to Culver, "You want me to get down and feel ahead for the black ice?"

Culver shook his head and said, "It's going straight in from here. No matter what happens."

When they were not more than two hundred yards from the ramp, they could easily make out through the slowly lifting mist the figures of the house crew setting up the final preparations for taking the buildings off the sled. A little off to one side they saw Millie standing in the soft rain, alternately watching the crew and the progress of the sled. At a hundred and fifty yards Culver and

Moose heard a crack like a rifle shot, and instantly Culver said, "Get down and look. It's from the back."

Moose was hardly off the bulldozer when he saw the cause of the sound. Not more than thirty yards behind the sled there was clear water. Over the whole path they had followed, the ice had cracked clear through to the water, and Moose stood unable to move for a few seconds as he tried to understand what he saw. The crack in the ice moved after them, as though it were some stalking animal. First it swerved a little to the right, then to the left, and then it came careening forward at twice the speed of the sled. Wherever it went, clear water followed directly behind it. Moose turned and ran a few yards to catch up with the bulldozer, yelling to Culver, "Give it everything it'll take or you're done for." He gestured toward the end of the sled. "It's all clear water back there."

"You go on," Culver said. He lifted his arm and waved Moose ahead. Moose stood for a moment unable to decide between staying with Culver and going on ahead. Then he was off and running toward the ramp.

Culver pushed the throttle of the bulldozer as far forward as it would go, and the machine groaned and shuddered as it picked up speed. But the vibrations it caused cancelled the effects of the increased speed, and the huge crack in the ice sprinted forward even faster. With less than seventy-five yards between him and the ramp, Culver realized that the ice ahead of him was a network of long white cracks. They looked almost like a huge group of arteries that had been made to supply the ice, and, from where he sat, he was just high enough to see them leap out before him as though they were multiplying geometrically. And farther along, where the ice touched the edge of the ramp, there was now a thin black line of clear water. The sight of it suddenly terrified Culver, and he knew that if it was more than a few inches wide there would be no way he could now get to the ramp. As he watched the ice continue to crack, he suddenly found that his terror had somehow boiled up into an anger ready to shoot from his body in all directions. He suddenly stood up in the cab and began to shout, "The crane line, the crane line! Heave it down the ramp!" He made wild gestures with his arms as though he might instantly explain what he wanted Moose to do. Again he yelled, "The goddamn crane line! Bring it down!" He was just about to repeat his sign language when he saw Moose suddenly bolt for the top of the ramp.

At thirty yards Culver saw that the line of water at the end of the ice was at least a foot wide, that if he kept going he would be in the water and the mud no more than a few feet from the end of the ramp. But beyond that he knew that there would be no way to stop the crushing momentum of the giant sled behind him. When he looked up from the water he saw Moose coming down the ramp with the line from the crane slung heavily over his shoulder. At the top of the ramp the crane stood poised and ready. Moose never broke stride when he got to the bottom of the ramp. With one long step he was back on the ice and moving toward the bulldozer faster than it was coming at him. From the start Moose knew what to do. Just when it appeared that the bulldozer would crush him flat, he jumped a little into the air and let himself be caught by the blade. For a second he looked stunned, but then he reached over with the hook from the crane and secured it to the steel frame of the machine. Then he slipped off and to the side and stumbled a little away from the machine and sled. Then he got control of himself and sprinted past the bulldozer and way on up the ramp.

In the cab Culver was still standing. With one hand in the air, alternately he judged the closing distance between him and the ramp and looked to see if the crane operator was ready. Then, suddenly, he was there. He

208

saw the blade and the front of the tracks of the bulldozer shoot out over the black water in front of the ramp, and at that moment he signaled the crane operator. When the cable from the crane snapped taut, it thrust the front end of the bulldozer into the air. Culver seemed for just an instant to lose his balance, and as the bulldozer lurched sharply to the left he had to grab one side of the rollbar to keep from going off. In the next instant the machine righted itself, and as the front end of it slammed down on the ramp, Culver dropped into the seat and hit the throttle. The bulldozer sprang forward without losing any of its speed, and when the front of the sled hit the ramp, the whole world shuddered. Then the sled was just onto the ramp, and its great weight suddenly caught the bulldozer and slowly reduced its speed and strength. When Culver realized that the bulldozer and sled were finally deadlocked, that the machine could pull the sled no farther up the ramp, he shut it off. He sat for a brief moment almost waiting to see if the sled would pull the bulldozer back down the ramp. When finally he was satisfied that the balance would last, he slowly got down from the cab and turned to look at the sled. Three-quarters of it was firmly on the ramp, the only portion of it jutting down into the black water being the part where Simmer's Garage had been.

During the next few moments Culver was completely turned in on himself. He stood looking at his immediate surroundings like an athlete who has thrust himself well past his exhaustion point. For a few minutes he did not know where he was; his gaze moved between the giant sled and the lake as though he were still trying to determine the chances of making the crossing. But then after a little while he began to look around almost as if he had suddenly found himself in some new and strange land. Even the people who stood watching him from the top of the ramp looked distant and strangely foreign. And beyond that Culver saw them standing motionless and watching him as though he were a freak. The men from the house crew stood in a tight little circle around the crane. Moose and Millie seemed to be standing together as one person, and beyond them were the state police cars with their red whirling lights. Then Culver's vision became slightly blurred, and for just an instant he thought he saw the people from the old town standing in a casual group just on the other side of the police cars. He blinked hard several times, but still the sight remained. He would have bet his last dollar that he was looking at Hal Bitterley, Calvin Runners, the Kellers, Jerky Barnhope, and even his own wife. But then, even though the sight was real enough to him, he knew that it was some ugly trick of his mind, and he dropped his gaze and slowly began to walk up the ramp. As he got to the top he saw that the state police had already broken out the equipment they would need to retrieve the bodies from the lake. Then he snapped completely around and, without even looking at anyone, started to walk off toward the new town.

Moose was the first to go after him, and Millie followed not more than fifty feet behind. Little by little they caught up to him, and for a long time the three of them walked together in silence. Finally, it was Millie who hooked an arm through Culver's and said, "Trying to do it was right. A long time from now people'll know that."

Culver stumbled a little but then righted himself and walked on. "So what," he said.

Seven

In the northern parts of New Hampshire, spring declares
itself in quiet little ways. There is a long period when it
only gives clues to its coming, the sky stays a heavy rolling gray, the snow cover slides back from the pastures
toward the heavy dark woods, and there seems always to
be a cold wet wind that slices in from the Atlantic. There
comes a time, usually in April, when it appears certain
that the death of the land is permanent, that in fact the
whole world has tipped over and winter is once again
about to roll in and take charge. Late winter snowstorms
seize the area, and for a day or two after one of them the
snow sits fresh and arrogant as though it knew it had
control of the towns and land. But real spring is there all
along—it is in the earth. From some pump buried miles
deep there comes a slow, insistent radiation that quietly
eats its way to the surface. It shows its power in the way
it deals with the late winter storms. It gets rid of them
from underneath. As though the ground were able to
turn itself into a warm sieve, the snow sags and dissipates
from underneath until once again the brown grass everywhere declares its authority.

It was a typical dead spring in the new town; the only
indication that it was not still winter was the lake. Within
a week after the crossing, most of the ice had gone out

of the lake, which looked to be in the process of heaving itself up around its banks. The runoff from the hills and the mountain came extremely fast, and at night in the new town the throaty rushings of the little streams could be heard everywhere. At the places where the streams ran into the lake they did so with a hard white force that disturbed the whole lake. It rose up in a muscled kind of force, as though it would topple over its banks and assault the whole area of the new town. In its way it appeared angered that it had been crossed, and when the cutting Atlantic wind swirled across it, whitecaps chattered along its surface like so many bared teeth.

But after two more weeks even the lake calmed itself, became less angry and somehow more mature than in the days immediately following ice-out. There was a feeling about the lake that its restlessness and anxiety were caused by the fact that neither Simmer's nor Sorenson's body had yet been found. The crew from the state police had been up and down the lake over and over, and they were genuinely baffled by not having discovered at least one of the bodies. During the first week Culver, Millie and Moose could not bring themselves to go anywhere near the lake, and when one or another of them had to drive past the end of it on an errand to Newfield, he did so quickly, eyes dead ahead on the road. But into the second week, after their houses were settled, after the post office and the town hall once more stood facing each other, it was as if they had all signed some spiritual agreement to keep watch for Simmer's body. All during the daylight hours one of the three of them was near the landing where Culver had brought in the sled. Sometimes, either by design or by accident, two of them kept watch. And occasionally during those days all three of them would be there staring out over the lake in a way that suggested they half expected Simmer to rise from the waters and join them.

When they were not keeping their vigil, each of them

had his own work in the new town. It was Moose's job to set, clean and reconnect all of the plumbing and heating lines in the buildings; Millie started three gardens; and Culver began construction of new chimneys on his house and the post office. Although there seemed among them a genuine warmth, an unspoken bond of closeness, clearly none of them was happy. They had done what even they had thought they could not do, and it was Culver who first realized that beyond the three of them there wasn't a soul who gave a good goddamn about it.

They found Simmer's body, or what was left of it, a week after they found Sorenson's. Simmer was clear at the other end of the lake when they found him in a balled-up position suspended about four feet below the surface. His body was so grossly misshapen that Culver had to confirm the identity for the police. And it was he who had to go to the Reverend Mr. Barker in Newfield to make the funeral arrangements.

As he stood in the vestibule of the huge and elegant church, his blood almost literally came afire at the thought that Simmer's funeral would have to be held in a place so gaudy and pretentious. And without really thinking about it, that was the first thing he said to Barker.

"You're welcome to take the services elsewhere," Barker told him. He looked like a man who had over the past several months suddenly gotten rich.

"There isn't any elsewhere," Culver answered.

"You know he can't be buried in our cemetery," Barker said. "The limitation requirement. I mean, he's never lived here."

"I've already staked an acre," Culver said, looking squarely at Barker.

"And the church fee?" Barker asked.

"You'll get what's yours."

"It must be accounted for," Barker told him.

"I don't doubt that."

"There's talk about you, you know," Barker suddenly flashed at Culver. "Talk that you've lost your wits."

"There's some truth to that," Culver said quietly.

"How many shall I anticipate for the service?"

Culver looked at Barker for a moment, and his face seemed suddenly wounded, as though Barker had in an instant gained complete control. "Three, anyway," Culver said.

"I'm not giving a funeral service for three people," Barker said.

"Yes, you are," Culver said.

"Not under any circumstances," Barker told him.

Culver looked hard at Barker for a moment and then he said, "You're absolutely correct. Carl Simmer's got no right being buried from a place like this. There's not a soul who'd say it's right."

"The man's got to have a service," Barker said quickly.

"He will," Culver answered. "And he'll have it from his own town hall."

Barker, suddenly enormously relieved, said, "I'll send my assistant."

"Well and good," Culver said, but he did not really hear Barker. In his mind there seemed to have come a lovely wave of peace, a feeling that he had, after all, done right.

The funeral was at one the next afternoon, and Culver, Moose and Millie got to the town hall just as the hearse came around the far bend in the road near the stand of pines. Following the hearse, Barker's assistant sat behind the wheel of a nine-year-old Volkswagen. He was a young man, not more than twenty-five, and for a moment Culver realized that it had been a long time since he had seen anyone under fifty. The young man stopped behind the hearse and got out of his car. He looked at the town hall for a moment and then turned and walked the little way to where Culver and the others stood beside Culver's truck. "Hadn't you'd better go with them?" Culver said to him. He gestured toward the undertakers, who were already wheeling Simmer's coffin up the walk.

"As I understand it," the young man said, "my job is to be with the living."

"Let's go on in," Culver said. Millie and Moose stepped a little aside and made room for the young man, and together the four of them went into the town hall.

When they entered, it seemed as if the whole building had in an instant changed its identity. Almost as though it had a will of its own it appeared to have become a solemn place, a gentle and quiet vault full of protection. The light sliced in through the windows on one side in soft muted shafts and spread through the building with a warm calm.

Simmer's coffin stood near the front, just below the stage, and as they approached it the undertakers moved away and back down the large center path between the folding chairs. Culver stepped back a little and let Millie and Moose sit down on the first row of chairs just to the left of the coffin. Then he sat in the chair closest to Simmer. The minister stood at the head of the coffin and looked out over the whole hall. Then he put his hands on the front of the coffin and looked directly at Culver, then at Moose and Millie. "Let us begin with a moment of silence," he said. On command they put their heads down, and there was no sound in the whole hall. The four of them looked statuelike and innocent, almost as though some wondrous sleep were about to spread through them all.

When they heard the first set of footsteps behind them they took no notice at all. Moose shifted a little in his seat, and Culver and Millie kept their eyes closed and down. But when the footsteps stopped a few rows behind them, they heard several other people shuffling one after another down the aisle. Then they too sorted themselves out, and their various sounds diminished as they stepped to their places and sat down. Culver turned slightly in his seat to look back over his shoulder. Then, in a violent double take, he snapped completely around. Three rows behind him sat Hal Bitterley and his wife. On the other side of the aisle and a few rows farther back Calvin Runners sat alone. Just behind him were the Graftons and the Lucarellis. Ned Hoffer was in his Oldenfield policeman's uniform just behind the Bitterleys, and behind him and a little to the right were the Woodmans. Not quite halfway down the aisle Mrs. Keller walked slowly, leaning heavily on her cane. Behind her, far in the back, was Bony James, his trousers covered with fresh dark earth stains from having just finished Simmer's grave.

Culver looked at each of them, and they in turn either nodded to him or raised a hand slightly. Then just as Culver turned around he heard Ellen begin to sing. Her voice at first came from the very back of the hall, but as it gained strength and clarity it somehow took possession of even the far dark corners of the building. Her voice seemed to Culver clearer and fresher than he had ever heard it, and as he listened he began to hum along quietly with her, as he had done many years before. When she had finished, the minister raised his head and said, "Let us begin."

When the service was over, the undertakers came down the aisle and stood by the coffin. "Leave him," Culver told them. They looked a little bewildered, but when Culver said, "He'll go in the truck," they walked away without looking back. Culver and Moose stood at one end of the coffin, and when Culver beckoned to Runners and Bitterley they came immediately and took the front end. The four men hoisted the coffin to their shoulders with what was clearly no effort. As they went down the aisle and out the small swinging doors, the others who had come followed. They dispersed slowly, as if they were simply leaving a town meeting, and then reappeared one by one in their trucks and cars in a small quiet line behind Culver's truck. Bitterley and Runners sat in the back of the truck with the coffin, and when the line was a good fifty yards long, Runners tapped on the back window for Culver to go.

The graveside service was short and full of calm, and when the minister finished they all stood and watched as Simmer's coffin was lowered and set finally in place. But even when Bony James began to ease the wet brown earth back into the grave, no one moved. It was as if they were waiting for some signal, some sign that would tell them it was all right to go.

The sign came from Culver, but he had not meant to give it. As he stood watching the dirt pile up around the coffin, his face began to look very old. For a moment his breathing became heavy, and then it seemed as though a great weight rested itself on his shoulders and back in one final test of his strength. It looked for a moment as though he would pitch forward into the grave, but just as Moose reached out an arm to him, he came erect wholly on his own. He turned, in fact snapped, himself away and free from everyone, and in one quick motion he was off and walking back toward the new town.

Those who stood by the grave seemed utterly frozen there, but then after a time it seemed that they had all arrived at some huge decision. At first it appeared as though one by one each of them had rejected the grave in front of him, and then as they turned and followed Culver, there was the feeling that in some way each of them had passed up through the grave, had in fact just risen out of the earth itself.

As if controlled by forces even they could not be aware of, those following Culver bunched up together in a little group not more than thirty or so yards behind him. Behind them Moose and Millie slowly brought up the rear.

The people approached the road that led up to the new town as though suddenly they had been injected with a mixture of great fear and great excitement.

The new town looked like Oldenfield, and yet it did not. Millie's store looked to be where it had always been; the post office and town hall, although not on any particular knoll, faced each other at the same distance they always had; and Culver's house around the bend was just visible through the thin line of trees along the new road. As the group walked on, those who had lived along the main street of the old town slipped quietly away as they passed the places where their houses had been. They seemed to go about the action without realizing what they were doing, as though the spaces where their houses had been were somehow magnetized and now sucked them back. Some of them, like Ellen and Calvin Runners, looked bewildered to be where they were, and others, like Hal Bitterley and his wife, looked as if they half-expected their houses to spring back to life in the next few seconds. The other people, those who had lived on the outskirts of Oldenfield, stood in small groups in front of Millie's store. Still others wandered up toward the post office.

It was Hal Bitterley who caught up to Culver first. He did not so much catch him as ease alongside him, and together they walked on without speaking. "By the fall," Bitterley said after a few moments, "we could have eight, maybe ten houses going up. There's a lot of us wanting our town back." He paused and looked out over the whole fresh place.

"Before we do anything," Culver said, "we'll hold town meeting."

"Within the week," Bitterley said.

But Culver did not really hear him. His eyes went past him to where Ellen was coming slowly up the new road. When she got to him he took her arm.

"Come on," he said, "let's go home."

218